The Cat Who
Went Bananas

Lilian Jackson Braun

The Cat Who Went Bananas

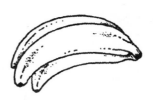

THORNDIKE
WINDSOR
PARAGON

This Large Print edition is published by Thorndike Press®, Waterville, Maine USA and by BBC Audiobooks, Ltd, Bath, England.

Published in 2005 in the U.S. by arrangement with G. P. Putnam's Sons, a division of Penguin Group (USA) Inc.

Published in 2005 in the U.K. by arrangement with Headline Book Publishing.

U.S. Hardcover 0-7862-7321-6 (Basic)
U.K. Hardcover 1-4056-1064-6 (Windsor Large Print)
U.K. Softcover 1-4056-2052-8 (Paragon Large Print)

The text of this Large Print edition is unabridged.
Other aspects of the book may vary from the original edition.

Set in 16 pt. Plantin by Minnie B. Raven.

Printed in the United States on permanent paper.

British Library Cataloguing-in-Publication Data available

Library of Congress Cataloging-in-Publication Data

Braun, Lilian Jackson.
    The cat who went bananas / by Lilian Jackson Braun.
        p. cm.
    ISBN 0-7862-7321-6 (lg. print : hc : alk. paper)
    1. Qwilleran, Jim (Fictitious character) — Fiction.
    2. Yum Yum (Fictitious character : Braun) — Fiction.
    3. Moose County (Imaginary place) — Fiction.   4. Koko
(Fictitious character) — Fiction   5. Country life — Fiction.
    6. Millionaires — Fiction.   7. Siamese cat — Fiction.
    8. Journalists — Fiction.   9. Cat owners — Fiction.   10. Cats —
Fiction.   11. Large type books.   I. Title.
PS3552.R354C3694 2005
    813'.54—dc22   2005002015

Dedicated to Earl Bettinger,
The Husband Who . . .

Acknowledgments

To Earl, my other half — for his husbandly love, encouragement, and help in a hundred ways.

To my research assistant, Shirley Bradley — for her expertise and enthusiasm.

To my editor, Natalee Rosenstein — for her faith in *The Cat Who* from the very beginning.

To my literary agent, Blanche C. Gregory, Inc. — for a lifetime of agreeable partnership.

To the real-life Kokos and Yum Yums — for their fifty years of inspiration.

Prologue

"Break a leg, Fran, honey!"

"Break a leg, Alden!"

"Break a leg, Derek, old boy!"

It was opening night of the new play in Pickax City (400 miles north of everywhere), and the actors were receiving the traditional bonhomie from well-wishers. The theatre club was doing Oscar Wilde's comedy of absurd upper-class manners: *The Importance of Being Earnest.*

Fran Brodie, interior designer, was playing Gwendolen. The male lead was being done by Alden Wade, a new man in town. Larry Lanspeak, owner of the department store, was perfect as the butler. And the unbearably haughty Lady Bracknell was being portrayed by Derek Cuttlebrink. It was not unusual for the role to be played by a male actor in drag; the difference here was that Derek, maître d' at an upscale restaurant, was six-feet-eight. Carol Lanspeak was directing. Jim Qwilleran would review the play.

ONE

Jim Qwilleran was primarily a columnist for the *Moose County Something*, but he was more. Previously a crime reporter for major dailies across the continent, he had relocated in the north country when he inherited the vast Klingenschoen fortune. This he immediately turned over to a philanthropic foundation, claiming that he felt uncomfortable with too much money. The K Fund, as it was called, improved schools, medical facilities, and the general quality of life in Moose County, leaving Qwilleran free to mix with the people, listen to their stories, write his column, and manage the care and feeding of two Siamese cats.

The three of them lived in a converted apple barn on the edge of Pickax City. It was there that Qwilleran was preparing their breakfast one day in September, arranging red salmon attractively on two plates with a garnish of crumbled Roquefort. (They were somewhat spoiled.) They sat on top of the bar in two identical bundles of fur, supervising the food preparation.

They were Koko and Yum Yum, well known to readers of the "Qwill Pen" column. The male was lithe, muscular, and cocky; the female smaller and softer and modest, although she could be demanding.

Both had the fawn fur, precise brown points, and blue eyes of the breed . . . as well as the Siamese tendency to voice an opinion on everything; Koko with a vehement "Yow!" and Yum Yum with a soprano "Now-ow!"

Just as Qwilleran was placing the two plates on the floor under the kitchen table, Koko's attention jerked away to a spot on the wall. A moment later the wall phone rang.

Before it could ring twice, Qwilleran said pleasantly into the mouthpiece, "Good morning."

"You're quick on the trigger, Qwill!" said the well-modulated voice of a woman he knew, Carol Lanspeak.

He explained, "I have an electronic sensor here. He tells me when the phone is going to ring and even screens incoming calls as acceptable or otherwise. What's on your mind, Carol?"

"Just wanted to ask if you're going to

11

write the program notes for the new production."

"Actually, I have another idea I'd like to discuss with you. Will you be in the store this morning?"

"All day! How about coffee and doughnuts at ten o'clock?"

"Not today," he said regretfully. "I've just had my annual physical, and Dr. Diane lectured me on my diet."

The Lanspeaks were a fourth-generation family in Moose County, dating back to pioneer days. Larry's grandmother ran a general store, selling kerosene, calico, and penny candy. Larry's father started the department store on Main Street. Larry himself, having acting talent, went to New York and had a little success, but then he married an actress and they came back to Pickax to manage the family business and launch a theatre club. Larry's daughter was the medical doctor who advised Qwilleran to consume more broccoli, less coffee — and one banana a day.

After taking leave of the cats, Qwilleran walked downtown to Lanspeak's Department Store. From the barnyard an unpaved road led through a dense patch of woods to the Park Circle, where Main Street divided around a small park. On its rim were two churches, the courthouse, the public library, and a huge block of fieldstone that had once been the Klingenschoen mansion.

Now it was a theatre for stage productions, and the headquarters of the Pickax theatre club. Northward, Main Street was a stretch of stone buildings more than a century old — now housing stores, offices, and the newly refurbished Mackintosh Inn.

The Lanspeaks' department store, which had started a century before, advertised "new-fashioned ideas with old-fashioned service."

Arriving there, Qwilleran walked between glass cases of jewelry, scarves, handbags, cosmetics, and blouses — to the offices in the rear, bowing to the clerks who hailed him: "Hi, Mr. Q. How's Koko, Mr. Q?"

He was known not only for his lively newspaper column and his philanthropy and his Siamese cats, but also for his magnificent pepper-and-salt moustache! It had not been equaled since Mark Twain visited Pickax in 1895. Qwilleran was a well-built six-feet-two, in his fifties, with a pleasing manner and a mellifluous voice. But it was his impressive moustache and brooding gaze that attracted attention. His photo appeared at the top of each "Qwill Pen" column.

Both Lanspeaks were working in the office.

Apart from their voice quality, there was nothing about the couple to mark them as actors. There was nothing striking about them, but onstage they could assume different personalities with professional skill. At the moment they were small-town storekeepers.

"Sit down, Qwill. I suppose you're well acquainted with our play," Larry said.

"We read it in college and went around talking like Lady Bracknell for the rest of the semester. Also, I've seen it performed a couple of times. It's a very stylish comedy. I'm curious to know why you scheduled it for this area — the boondocks, if you'll pardon the expression."

"Good question!" Larry replied. "Ask *her!* Wives sometimes rush in where husbands fear to tread."

Throwing a humorous smirk in his direction, Carol explained, "The club presents one classic play every year, and Larry and I happen to agree that Oscar Wilde is one of the wittiest playwrights who ever lived. The Lockmaster group did this play at the Academy of Arts two years ago. Superb! And Alden Wade, who played Jack Worthing, has just relocated in Pickax and joined the theatre club. He's terrifically talented and good-looking!"

"What brought him to Moose County?" Qwilleran asked.

"The tragic loss of his wife," Carol said. "He needed a drastic change of scene. It's definitely our gain. And since he has sold his property — a horse farm, I believe — it looks as if he intends to stay."

"That guy," Larry interrupted, "does the stylized upper-crust Jack Worthing so well that the rest of the cast is finding it contagious!"

"We had trouble casting the role of Algernon," Carol went on, "so Alden suggested Ronnie Dickson, who played the role in Lockmaster and was willing to help out, even though it's a sixty-mile round-trip drive for every rehearsal — and he hasn't missed a single one."

"Which is more than I can say for our own people," Larry added. "Now all we need to worry about is the audience. They'll be hearing perfectly straight-faced actors speaking outrageous lines. How will they react? I know a few who'll call it silly — and walk out."

Carol said, "Most people in Moose County like a laugh, but will they get the point? I'm wondering, Qwill, if you could write the program notes with that in mind."

"Precisely why I am here! I've noticed that our audiences never read the program notes before the show; they're too busy chatting with people they know in the surrounding seats. What they should know — in order to enjoy the play to the fullest — is not read until they get home. So here's my idea: Tuesday, to be exact, I'll devote the Qwill column to an explanation of the Oscar Wilde style."

"I like the idea!" Carol cried. "Everyone reads the 'Qwill Pen,' and you have a way of educating people without their knowledge."

"True!" Larry said. "The locals have a sense of humor; it's simply a matter of getting them tuned in. Give him a script of the play, Carol."

With the conference ended, Carol walked with Qwilleran to the front door, and Larry plunged into a stack of paperwork.

She asked, "Is Polly Duncan excited

about changing jobs?"

"She's saddened to be leaving the library after twenty-odd years as director, but challenged by the prospect of managing a bookstore. Do you have anything to suggest as a graduation present? She has enough jewelry."

"We're expecting a shipment of lovely cashmere robes, including a heavenly shade of blue that Polly would love."

Qwilleran's footsteps never led him directly home. There was always a need to buy toothpaste at the drugstore or look at neckties in the men's shop. Today his curiosity led him to Walnut Street to view the new bookstore being bankrolled by the Klingenschoen Fund.

Across the street, a vacant lot that had long been the eyesore of Pickax City had been purchased by the K Fund. Its tall weeds and slum of abandoned buildings had been replaced by a park, and beyond that, a complex of studio apartments at rents affordable to young singles employed in stores and offices downtown. It was called Winston Park. With the coming of the bookstore, the entire commercial neighborhood was getting a face-lift.

★ ★ ★

Qwilleran wrote his Tuesday column in the style his readers liked.

Expect the unexpected, friends, when you go to see the new play. *The Importance of Being Earnest* is said to be the masterpiece of the nineteenth-century playwright and wit Oscar Wilde.

It's a comedy of manners — a spoof on the snobbish upper-crust society in London. According to director Carol Lanspeak, it calls for stylized acting, not realism. Their self-important posturing goes with their lofty opinions. Example:

"To lose one parent, Mr. Worthing, may be regarded as a misfortune. To lose both looks like carelessness."

The plot is wacky, if not totally insane. One young bachelor has invented a wicked brother named Ernest, another has invented an invalid relative named Bunbury. Why? You'll have to see the play.

Figuring prominently in the plot is a handbag — not a woman's purse, but a small piece of luggage, just large enough to carry. . . . You'll have to wait and see!

Then there's the matter of cucumber

sandwiches! A young gentleman sends out invitations to an afternoon tea and orders cucumber sandwiches as refreshments. They are so good that he eats the whole plateful before the guests arrive.

I asked food writer Mildred Riker what is so special about cucumber sandwiches. She said, "To make the classic sandwich, cut a round of bread, spread it with softened butter, layer it with crisp cucumbers sliced paper-thin, and top it with another round of buttered bread. They're delicious! You can't stop eating them!"

Some of the playwright's witticisms are still being used today:

"Thirty-five is a very attractive age. London is full of women of the highest society who have remained thirty-five for years."

Every evening at eleven o'clock, Qwilleran put a cap on the day by phoning Polly Duncan, the chief woman in his life. On this night she sounded weary.

"You've been working long hours again!" he chided her.

"There's so much to do!" she cried. "I spend mornings at the library and then

19

seven or eight hours at the bookstore."

"You must shake loose and come to the opening night of the new play. I know you like Wilde."

"Oh dear! That's the night of the library board's farewell banquet for me!"

"Well, that's important. We'll catch it later. They're doing the play for three weekends. But I'll miss you on opening night. Everyone will ask about you."

There followed scraps of the unimportant news exchanged by persons who have known each other for a long time.

"You should drink a cup of cocoa and go to bed," he finally advised. "Is there anything I can do for you tomorrow?"

"Yes," she said promptly. "You could pick up Dundee!"

TWO

Dundee was a marmalade cat named after the Scottish city famous for marmalade. As a kitten he had been donated to the new bookstore being built in Pickax — as a mascot, a bibliocat. He had an outgoing personality that would make friends and influence customers. His luscious tabby markings were cream and apricot, and his eyes were a lively green.

A small apartment in a corner of the office awaited him, equipped with basket-bed, feeding station, water bowl, and "facilities," as Polly called them.

She explained to Qwilleran, "We think he should get acquainted with his new environment now, while friendly staffers are setting it up — and before the squealing customers arrive."

The breeder was the wife of Kip MacDiarmid, editor in chief of the *Lockmaster Ledger* and a friend of Qwilleran's. They met frequently for lunch at Inglehart's in Lockmaster.

That was where they had lunch on the day of the Dundee Expedition, as Qwilleran would later call it in his personal journal.

While driving to Lockmaster, he reminisced about Winston, the dust-colored longhair with plumed tail who did the dusting in the late Eddington Smith's dusty old bookshop. Customers went into the shop to say hello to Winston and always bought a pre-owned book for a couple of dollars. Most, if not all, of Qwilleran's books came from Edd's shop before arson reduced it to ashes. Winston had escaped and taken shelter in the weed-covered vacant lot that would now be a park bearing his name. His full name was Winston Churchill, but it was not generally known that he was named after the American author and not the British prime minister.

As soon as they were seated in the restaurant, Kip said in his usual bantering style, "I see you guys in the boondocks are up to your old tricks, stealing our best people. First you lure our doctors, then our weatherman, and now Alden Wade!"

Qwilleran's retort was prompt. "We can't

help it if they find our quality of life superior."

"Seriously," Kip said, "Alden is a sad case. Do you remember the sniping incident last year? The victim was Alden's wife!"

"The case was never closed. He was surrounded by the sad voices and sad faces of sympathizers. Then their son was no longer around so he sold their big house and went in search of a new scene."

"Can't blame him," Qwilleran said. "I've never met him, but I understand he's joined the theatre club. That'll be therapeutic."

The waitress arrived to take their orders and placed a bud vase with a single yellow rose in the middle of the table. "The boss wants you to enjoy this with your lunch. It's in its fourth day."

"Tell Miss Inglehart we're honored," Kip said solemnly.

They placed their orders, and then Qwilleran asked, "Kip, dare I ask the significance of the yellow rose?"

"You don't know! Moose County is more backward than I thought. Rose-watching is the current fascination around here. Once a week everyone buys a single long-stemmed rose in the bud and watches it unfurl day by day."

"Then Lockmaster County is loonier than I thought," was Qwilleran's verdict. "Who started it? The Florists' Association? What is the purpose? Do the rose-watchers compare notes on the Internet? Is there a prize?"

"Moira knows more about it than I do. Ask her when you pick up Dundee."

The sandwiches were served. The house specialty at lunchtime was the French dip with fries, and silence fell on the table for a while.

Then Qwill asked, "How's your daughter doing at J school, Kip?"

"Fine! Kathie loves it! She's got journalism in her genes. She and her boyfriend, Wesley, were supposed to enroll at State this fall, you know, but he dropped out. Too bad. They both wrote for the school paper and had part-time jobs at the *Ledger*. He was a good kid. Top grades, no bad habits. I envisioned him as a future son-in-law, with the two of them taking over the *Ledger* when I retire. It's no *Washington Post*, but it's a respected country newspaper. All it lacks is the 'Qwill Pen' column. We'd put it on the front page if you'd syndicate, Qwill."

"It wouldn't work," Qwilleran protested.

"Most of my columns are of local, topical interest in Moose County."

"Nothing wrong with that," the editor said. "It could be the beginning of a healthy link between our two counties — instead of the mutual snobbery that keeps us apart. Both counties could benefit. Think about it. Are you having dessert?"

The MacDiarmids lived in a planned neighborhood, circa 1940, of two-story colonials with attached garages on cozy cul-de-sacs. There was nothing like that in Moose County. On the way there, Qwilleran recalled Polly's comment: "Be prepared for a much more vivacious Moira since she has her career as cat breeder and their daughter has gone away to college. She's dropped the wife-and-mother role."

When he arrived, Moira flung open the door and cried, "Come in! Come in! Dundee is ready to go — along with his impedimenta. He's downstairs in the cattery, saying good-bye to his confreres. Go and sit in the family room, Qwill. I'll bring him up, and the two of you can get acquainted before you take off."

Qwilleran, meanwhile, could hear Moira's falsetto pep talk to the marmalade brood below.

When she reappeared she was preceded by a handsome marmalade yearling. He had the leanness of youth, the greenest of green eyes, and a cocky swagger. He went directly to Qwilleran's chair and checked out the famous moustache.

"Yours is the first moustache he's ever seen," Moira said. "He has a wonderful, outgoing, fearless personality." Then to the cat she said, "This is your uncle Qwill, Dundee! He's going to take you to a bookstore where you'll be the official bibliocat."

"Is there anything I should tell Polly?"

"We've been in touch by phone regularly. She's as excited as we are! He'll travel in his own carrier and take his own favorite scratching post. It's covered in green carpet. She has a basket-bed for him, but we're sending his own cushion for it."

At this point, Dundee jumped on Qwilleran's lap and presented him with a small rag doll, well chewed and still damp.

"Isn't that sweet?" Moira said. "He's giving you Rebecca, his favorite toy! Polly said we should send all his familiar playthings. He even has an old toothbrush that he dearly loves. He parades around importantly with it clamped crosswise in his little jaws. . . . Now let's talk about something else and ignore him for a while."

"For starters," Qwilleran said, "tell me about rose-watching. Is it a joke?"

"Not at all! You should introduce it in your column, Qwill. It's a simple, private way of calming the nerves in these days of terrorists and snipers."

"Are you a rose-watcher, Moira?"

"Definitely. And Kip finds it an aid to problem-solving; it clears the mind."

Hmmm, Qwilleran mused; that faker never admitted he watched roses! Casually, he asked Moira, "Do you think Alden Wade is a rose-watcher?"

"That poor man! It would help him, I know. And to make things worse, when his stepson came home for the funeral, there was a nasty scene at the funeral home, and the boy stomped out. Kathie hasn't heard from him since. She says he never got along with his stepfather. Wesley idolized his real dad and resented it when his mom married so soon."

Qwilleran said, "So apparently Alden married an older woman."

"Yes, but you'd never guess it. She was a horsewoman and in excellent condition. . . . All of this is confidential, of course."

"Of course."

★ ★ ★

Driving back to Pickax with a contented cat in the carrier beside him, Qwilleran pulled off the road to phone Polly at the library and was told she had left early to handle an emergency at the bookstore.

He phoned the bookstore. "I've got him!" he reported. "We've just crossed the county line. We'll be there in twenty-eight minutes."

"Is he nervous?" she asked anxiously.

"Not as nervous as I am. He lounges in his carrier and doesn't say a word. No yowling! No shrieking!"

"He'll be a good bibliocat. Did Moira send some of his things?"

"Yes. His cushion . . . and his scratching post . . . and his toothbrush. See you shortly. Roll out the red carpet."

The new bookstore occupied the site of Eddington Smith's quaint shop, where he had sold pre-owned books, done bookbinding in the back room, and kept a bibliocat in sardines. It was a strange piece of property — a block long but squeezed between Book Alley and Walnut Street — a miscalculation on the part of the founding fathers, it was said, after too much fish-house punch.

The new bookstore had to be long and narrow, but it turned its back to Book Alley, had parking lots at both ends, and faced the park across Walnut Street. The exterior was gray stucco to harmonize with the old stone buildings of Pickax, but it had a red tile roof, and the name of the store was spelled out in block letters of aluminum mounted directly on the gray stucco:

THE PIRATE'S CHEST

The entrance doors, flanked by display windows, were in the center of the building. Inside, there were books to the right and books to the left, but straight ahead was a wide, inviting staircase leading to the lower level and — mounted on the wall above it — a real pirate's chest of ancient wood with iron straps. It had been buried on the property for a century and a half.

Staffers in green smocks were still unpacking books and stocking the shelves when Qwilleran walked in with the cat carrier, but they swarmed around, crying, "Here he is! Here's Dundee! . . . Isn't he gorgeous?"

"Don't overwhelm him!" Polly said. "Take him into the office, Qwill, and let him wander out when he feels like it."

Half an hour later, Dundee made his formal appearance. He had inspected his quarters, had a bit to eat, tested the "facilities," and then walked confidently into the selling area, with his toothbrush clamped firmly between his jaws.

Late that evening before Qwilleran could phone Polly, she called him. "I'm going to bed early and turning the phone off. I didn't want you to worry." Only once before had he seen her push herself too far, and she had landed in the hospital.

"But I am definitely worried about you, Polly. Make up your mind to phase out the library. They'll never let you go if you don't cut the cord. And one more thing. Don't — set — your — alarm — clock!"

"I won't, dear. Thank you, dear."

THREE

"Your uncle George is coming," Qwilleran said to the Siamese as he brushed their silky coats. "Be on your best behavior. Mind your manners. Don't interrupt conversations with irrelevant remarks."

The more one speaks to cats, the smarter they become, Qwilleran believed. What one says to them doesn't matter; it's the tone that counts: serious, purposeful.

Uncle George was a private joke. A new attorney from Down Below, named George Barter, had joined the prestigious Hasselrich law firm to represent Qwilleran in all matters concerning the Klingenschoen Fund. In a slip of the tongue the WPKX announcer identified the new attorney as "George Breze . . . uh, correction: George Barter." Once more WPKX had slipped on a banana peel: George Breze was a local character of dubious integrity, a certified oddball. He was once quoted as saying, "Why should I learn to read and write? I can hire somebody to do it."

After the WPKX faux pas, the jokers in the coffee shops guffawed for a week, and the attorney changed his business cards to "G. Allen Barter."

He would henceforth be known to locals as Allen, although he would always be George to the IRS and Social Security.

His conferences with Qwilleran were held at the latter's apple barn. Bart, as Qwilleran called him, maintained that a visit to the barn was always like a shot in the arm.

It was a century-old apple barn — octagonal and forty feet high. A fieldstone foundation and wood-shingled siding had a mellow old patina in contrast to the bleached wood beams of the interior.

Business started that morning with Bart's report on financial and legal affairs of the K Fund, which Qwilleran found tiresome, although he was careful to conceal his reaction.

Then it was his turn to report: The Pirate's Chest was beginning to look like a bookstore. It would be ready to open in another week. The bibliocat had moved in and acted as if he owned the place. Polly had hired an assistant with bookstore credentials. Part-time helpers were available when and if needed, happy to be associated with The Pirate's Chest.

"Believe it or not," Qwilleran said, "there are crackpots — like me — who would work for the sheer joy of working with words and ideas and adventures in hardcover bindings."

Bart said, "You should write a column on that, Qwill."

"I did. Before you came here. It was actually a tribute to Edd Smith. Books were his life. Although he never sat down and read one, he consulted books, collected them, sold them, talked about them, and repaired them." Qwilleran paused, remembering the little gray man, his dusty shop, and his dingy living quarters in the rear, which he shared with bookbinding equipment, the ever-present aroma of sardines and clam chowder, the cracked mirror above a rusty sink, and the handgun on the shelf beneath.

"Anyway," Qwilleran went on, "volunteers are falling all over each other to participate in the Edd Smith Place on the lower level. They call themselves Edd Smith's People and wear ESP badges. It occupies half the lower level; the rest is earmarked for special events."

"Of what nature?"

"Book reviews, a children's storybook hour, a literary club, and so forth. There is a new man in town who has been hired to handle these on a part-time basis. His name is Alden Wade, and he's just moved here from Lockmaster following the murder of his wife by a sniper's bullet."

Bart recalled the case. "Did they ever find the perpetrator?"

"No, and survivors suffer more when there is no closure. Alden came here to get away from it all. Working at the bookstore and joining the theatre club will be therapeutic. You'll see him in the Oscar Wilde play, if you go."

"We have tickets for Saturday night."

"And apropos of that, Bart, I think it's time the K Theatre had a better name."

He was talking about the giant cube of fieldstone that had been the Klingenschoen mansion before being gutted by fire. Now it was a theatre for stage productions.

"I agree that the name lacks imagination," the attorney said.

"It sounds like a breakfast cereal to me," Qwilleran said, "or the index tab of an office file folder."

"What would you suggest?"

"Something like Theatre Arts in the same type of signage used on the bookstore and the Mackintosh Inn. There could be classes in acting, voice control, and so forth."

"Who could teach?"

"This same Alden Wade who's playing the lead in the new play."

"You've done your homework," Bart said. "I'll move it forward."

Little did Uncle George know that Koko had been staring at Qwilleran during the rush of ideas. Qwilleran agreed with the eighteenth-century poet Christopher Smart, who maintained that cats have a way of placing ideas in human heads — not only reminders about food.

"Meanwhile, tell me what's going on at Winston Park. I've seen the trucks, and I can't figure out what they're doing."

Qwilleran explained with limited enthusiasm, "It's an idea dreamed up by those eggheads in Chicago; it remains to be seen how it goes over with the folks in the so-called boondocks. The park is based on such practicalities as weather, maintenance, and human behavior.

"First, we're in the deep-freeze zone, so a fountain in the middle of the park would be turned off five months of the year. Instead, they propose *a piece of statuary* as the focal point. Only Polly knows what it is, and she's not talking, except to say that it's tall and vertical."

Bart said, "I hope it's not an unclothed

human figure. It wouldn't be well received, I'm afraid."

"That remains to be seen. It'll be shrouded in tarpaulin until the unveiling at the press preview. Are you prepared for the experts' Decision Number Two? *No park benches!* They attract loafers and picnickers, who leave beer cans and lunch wrappings around instead of putting them in the trash containers, which are inevitably filled to overflowing."

"Hmmm," the attorney murmured thoughtfully.

"Decision Number Three: *Ground cover instead of grass,* which needs mowing and raking seven months of the year. Also, evergreens instead of deciduous trees, which are leafless much of the year and responsible for a leaf problem every fall."

"Is there any good news?"

"Yes, we'll play it up in the paper as something new and different: *a walking-and-learning park!* Walking paths will curve around between the evergreens, which will represent many varieties — some new to local tree buffs — and all will be labeled. Speakers will be provided for garden clubs, and teachers will bring their classes and then give tests — with prizes for the highest scores, and photos of the winners in the newspaper."

"I hope the experts know what they're doing," Bart said. "Good-bye, cats!"

"Yow!" Koko replied. He had a limited vocabulary but there was variety in his intonation. It could be agreeable, critical, apologetic, demanding, outraged, or alarming.

Bart gathered up his papers and left, followed by two cats interested in speeding the departing guest. Their noontime snack was overdue.

That evening after dinner, the three residents of the apple barn assembled for a reading session. Qwilleran had only to shout "Read!" and the Siamese came running: Yum Yum to take possession of his lap, Koko to select a title. He was the designated bibliocat, and seemed to take his responsibility seriously.

All available wall space was covered with bookshelves, and until recently they had been filled to capacity with pre-owned books purchased from the late Eddington Smith. In selecting a book, Koko would prance back and forth, then stop and look up at the shelves, make his decision, crouch, and spring! His powerful hind legs catapulted him to the right height, as much as seven feet above the floor. Never did he overshoot his goal or fall short; his spatial instinct was amazing to Qwilleran, who was a slave to a tape measure.

Then Koko would squeeze behind the books, sniffing the pages until he found a title he wanted (no need to read the printing on the spine). Bumping it with his nose, he would knock it off the shelf. Ideally, Qwilleran was there to catch it and that was the choice for the reading.

Recently there had been some empty shelf space, since a hundred books had been donated to the Edd Smith Place. A small army of volunteers had collected books from libraries around the county. Volunteers would staff the shop, and proceeds would benefit the Literacy Council and an Edd Smith scholarship.

Donated books, in order to be accepted, had to meet the requirements of the ESP. Food-spotted cookbooks and eighth-grade algebra books did not qualify.

When the Edd Smith Place opened, Qwilleran would be the first customer.

Opening night at the K Theatre was a pleasant tradition that both Polly and Qwilleran enjoyed, but her work overload had sapped her energy and enthusiasm. Regretfully, he attended without her.

Qwilleran had no objection to attending opening night alone, when he was reviewing the play. He could use the solitude to marshal his opinions and devise catchy phrases.

Purposely he arrived at the theatre late, parking in the space reserved for the press. The audience was already seated and the houselights were beginning to dim when he strode down the aisle and slipped into the critic's traditional seat in row five.

There was a moment of silent anticipation, and then the curtain rose slowly, and during the breathless stillness Qwilleran heard two whispering voices behind him.

"That's Mr. Q."

"He's gonna write it up for the paper."

"He's alone."

"Where's his friend?"

"Maybe they broke up."

The scene onstage was a posh bachelor flat in nineteenth-century London. A butler with painfully rigid dignity entered in slow motion, carrying a silver platter of cucumber sandwiches.

The whisperer in row six said, "He owns the department store."

When the glamorous Gwendolen entered, it was whispered, "Her dad's the police chief."

Everyone in the immediate vicinity was restless with annoyance, and Qwilleran wondered how to squelch the commentary without resorting to violence. Then one of the actors spoke some pithy lines in a rich baritone, and the voice said, "That's him! That's him! His wife was shot!"

And a booming voice in the same row bellowed, *"Shut up!"*

The whispering stopped. The dialogue onstage never missed a beat. And the audience went on responding to the witty lines and ludicrous characters with chuckles and murmurs of delight. Lady Bracknell, with a Queen Mary hat adding inches to her height, was received with quiet amusement.

During intermission, when Qwilleran went to the lobby to stretch his legs, he met the Comptons at the drinking fountain. Lyle was superintendent of schools; Lisa was a retired educator now serving as volunteer captain of the Edd Smith People.

Lyle said, "What did you think of the fracas in the sixth row? No wonder Lockmaster people think we're barbarians in Moose County."

Lisa said, "That was our intrepid Ernie

Kemple who came to the rescue. It took nerve to do what he did, but it didn't faze the members of the cast."

Qwilleran said, "Actors can't afford to be distracted by disturbances in the audience. Once I was onstage with an actress in Noel Coward's *Private Lives* and a loud guffaw in the front row made her forget her lines — completely! I'll never forget that experience, and it was thirty years ago!" The lobby lights blinked. He added quickly, "Lisa, could you meet me at the bookstore for an interview about the ESP?"

"I'll be there all day tomorrow."

They returned to the auditorium.

The two seats behind Qwilleran remained vacant for the rest of the show.

How Polly would have enjoyed the play! In a way it was his own fault that she was not there, he decided. He should never have had the K Fund underwrite a bookstore for Polly to manage. He had suggested it only because she was disenchanted with her work at the library. She had allowed herself to be consumed by the new challenge.

He missed dining out with Polly two or three times a week . . . weekend walks on the lakeshore and on the banks of the

Ittibittiwassee, and evenings of classical music at the apple barn, where the music system was superb and the acoustics were fabulous. Once, he recalled, they were dining at the Grist Mill and spent ten minutes discussing the meaning of "perspicuity" and "perspicacity"; then they skipped dessert in order to hurry home and consult *Webster's Unabridged*. Should they go to her place or his place?

She had the newest edition, the third; he had the second edition, which he really preferred. He had bought the third edition, he explained, but it was in the cats' quarters, where they used it as a scratching pad.

Soon, Qwilleran now hoped, his life with Polly would return to normalcy. He went home and had a large dish of ice cream — diet or no diet.

FOUR

On Saturday morning Qwilleran walked to the bookstore to interview Lisa Compton — through the patch of woods in his property, up Main Street, and around behind the post office. In motor-minded Pickax, he was a familiar sight in his orange baseball cap. For him it was a safeguard — not only in traffic but in the woods, where a predatory owl might otherwise mistake his good head of hair for furry prey.

The bookstore turned its back to the post office loading docks and faced Walnut Street — a gray stucco edifice blending with the century-old stone buildings of the city. Double doors opened into a vestibule with a large doormat, obligatory in a town called the Buckle of the Snow Belt. Custom-imprinted, the mat did not say "Welcome to The Pirate's Chest" or "Please Wipe Your Feet" but . . . "Don't Let the Cat Out!"

For further practical reasons it had been decided to carpet the interior in charcoal gray instead of a lively green to match the bibliocat's magical eyes, but lively green smocks on the personnel were an acceptable compromise. They bustled about their bookish chores, but there was no sign of Polly. Either she had taken his advice and slept late or she had ignored his advice and was putting in a few more hours at the library.

Neither surmise was true. "Mrs. Duncan is out having her hair done," Qwilleran was informed. "Mrs. Compton is waiting for you downstairs."

There was nothing downbeat about "downstairs" at the bookstore. One experienced a sense of majesty in walking down the broad staircase, stepping on the wide treads, and gazing up at the pirate's chest on the wall above — the real chest, which had been buried on the site since the 1850s.

To the right was the flexible suite of meeting rooms. To the left was Edd Smith's Place. Volunteers wearing green vests with the ESP logo busied themselves at the computer, on the stepladder, or at other tasks made enjoyable by Dundee's presence. Lisa Compton made introductions and then whisked Qwilleran away to a meeting room, where he taped the following:

44

What was the first book in the history of Moose County? Make a guess.

Probably a prayer book belonging to a pastor who came here with his flock. The early settlers were intrepid and hardworking, but few were literate. Even in the boom years, the owner of all the sawmills along the coast could neither read nor write. In the late nineteenth century wealthy families built mansions with impressive libraries, the status symbol of the day. The shelves were filled with leather-bound, gold-tooled books that they would never read. Then, in the twentieth century a middle class emerged, and they read for pleasure.

What did they read?

The classics — but also the new romances, mysteries, adventure stories. They bought books on art, poetry, and etiquette. Edd Smith's father sold books door-to-door for nickels and dimes. These are the books that are being donated to the ESP today.

How does the ESP work?

The Pirate's Chest has allocated half of the lower level for the Edd Smith Place. Volunteers, called the Edd Smith People, will staff the shop, and proceeds go to the Literacy Council and the annual Eddington Smith scholarships.

Are folks donating enough books to stock the shelves?

Well! For starters there was the front-page announcement that a prominent citizen had donated a hundred books. Although no name was mentioned, everyone guessed it was you and wanted to participate. Volunteers have also solicited books from acquaintances, picked them up, and catalogued them. In memory of Eddington Smith . . . that dear little man! Everyone wants to carry on his work!

Isn't it a formidable task, managing this operation, Lisa?

I couldn't do it without a dedicated board of directors. They help me make decisions, solve problems, and maintain enthusiasm among the volunteers. Burgess Campbell, Maggie Sprenkle, Dr. Abernethy, and Violet Hibbard. I'm deeply grateful for their support.

Qwilleran turned off the tape recorder. "I've never met Violet Hibbard," he said in an aggrieved tone. As a journalist, he expected to know everyone and everything on his beat.

46

"She's a wonderful woman, recently retired after a career teaching English lit in eastern colleges."

"How old is she?"

"About our age. She took early retirement when she inherited the Hibbard House. She's the last of the Hibbards, and a developer wanted to buy it, tear it down, and build condos. The thought of it makes me shudder! Do you know the Hibbard mansion, Qwill?"

"I know where it is, but I've never seen it. I understand it's been pictured in national magazines."

"Yes. In a county filled with stone mansions, it's built entirely of wood, and miraculously it has survived forest fires, lightning, arson and accidents with wood-burning stoves and fireplaces, and human carelessness. Violet has undertaken to preserve it as a high-class guest house. . . . There's a story for you, Qwill. And Violet would love to meet you. She adores your column!"

Qwilleran automatically liked readers who adored his column. With a nonchalant shrug he said, "Give me a ring when she's going to be in the shop. I'll drop in."

 When Qwilleran walked home from the bookstore and emerged from the woods, Koko was doing his jumping-jack act in the kitchen window. It meant that there was a message on the answering machine. Sure enough, the red light was blinking, and the message was from Wetherby Goode, the WPKX meteorologist (real name: Joe Bunker).

"Hey, Qwill! This is Joe. Did Polly tell you the latest from Indian Village? I'll pop in on my way to the studio and we'll shoot the breeze. Will you be there around four-thirty? Leave a yes or no on the answer box."

Qwilleran's answer was yes. What was the news that Polly hadn't told him?

Indian Village was an upscale residential area outside the city limits: rustic condos and apartment clusters in a wooded setting. There were nature trails along the Ittibittiwassee River, and there was a clubhouse with a bar, a bridge club, an occasional lecture, and a bird-watcher's society.

In the winter when the apple barn was impossible to heat, Qwilleran lived in Unit Four of a strip of condos called the Willows. Wetherby was his next-door neighbor, along with his cat, Jet Stream. Polly lived in Unit One with her Brutus and Catta. For a while Unit Two had been occupied by an ailurophobe, but he left suddenly. "Allergic to cat hair," his neighbors said with a wink. There was more to the story than they cared to discuss.

When Wetherby "popped in" at four-thirty, they sat at the bar, and he had a beer while Qwilleran had a ginger ale, asking, "Did you see the play last night, Joe?"

"Yeah! They did a swell job! I imagine it was a challenge for the actors, but Carol is a great director."

"Did you hear the commotion in the audience at the beginning?"

"Sure did! Only Ernie Kemple would have the guts to shut them up the way he did. He has a voice like a foghorn."

Qwilleran said, "Apparently, the culprits were offended; they didn't return for the second act."

"Well, you know, Qwill, people get used to talking while watching TV, and they think it's okay to do it at the theatre. They left because their feelings were hurt."

Koko jumped on the adjoining bar stool as if wanting to join in the conversation.

"How's Jet Stream?" Qwilleran asked.

"He wants to know when you guys are moving back to the Village."

"Usually the first of November. . . . But what's the big news? Did the bird-watchers spot a yellow-bellied sapsucker?"

"The scuttlebutt is that Unit Two has been purchased — by Alden Wade! Better lock up your girlfriend! He has a reputation as a lady-killer."

Why had Polly not mentioned this? Qwilleran wondered. She was always the first to hear a rumor. But calmly he remarked, "It's about time they found a buyer for Unit Two. It downgrades a neighborhood if a property is vacant too long. . . . Another drink, Joe?"

"No thanks. I've got to amble over to the station."

"I hope the new neighbor likes cats," Qwilleran said, making light of the situation.

He wondered, after Wetherby had driven away, if Polly had been the one who suggested Unit Two to the personable widower who was going to work at the bookstore part-time, and who was said to be a lady-killer. Wetherby was a native of Lockmaster. He should know.

The Siamese were standing shoulder to shoulder, waving their tails in unison — a polite reminder that it was dinnertime.

Qwilleran said, "How would you guys like to move back to the Village earlier this year?"

He spent the evening writing his review for Monday's paper, being careful not to praise the two actors from Lockmaster more than hometown members of the theatre club. He also consulted his watch frequently.

At ten o'clock he phoned Polly. There was no answer. He left a message.

He had given the cats their bedtime treat and escorted them to their suite on the third balcony when Polly called. Her exhilaration was a far cry from her previous weariness.

"Qwill! You'll never guess where I've been tonight! To the Oscar Wilde play! Since Alden, one of our staffers, is in the cast, I thought it appropriate to take the Green Smocks, as we call the girls, to see the show. My treat! They loved it! They had all read your Tuesday column, stimulating their interest." She paused for breath.

He said, "I'm glad to see you recovered from last night's doldrums. Do we credit Oscar Wilde or your hairdresser?"

"Both!" she said with a trilling laugh that he had not heard for some time — not since she had started studying her encyclopedic manual on how to run a bookstore.

Before he could comment, she asked, "How was your interview with Lisa Compton?"

"Quite enlightening. There are some things I'd like to discuss with you. How about Sunday brunch at Tipsy's tomorrow and then a musicale at the barn? I have a new recording of 'La Symphonie Fantastique' that you'll like."

"Well . . . I really should get out my winter wardrobe and prepare for cold weather."

"Smart idea! I'm thinking of moving back to the Village earlier because of the weather forecast. . . . By the way, I hear that Unit Two is being purchased."

She hesitated before saying, "Oh, really?" It was her all-purpose expression indicating uneasiness, suspicion, alarm, and a desire to evade the subject.

"I don't know who it is, except that it's a single man. I hope he likes cats," he added in jest.

"Where did you hear it?" she asked — defensively, he thought.

"I don't recall. Either at the theatre Friday night or at the bookstore today. It will be good to have the unit occupied. I hope he's congenial. . . . Well, sleep well. À bientôt!"

"*À bientôt*," she echoed with a noticeable lack of spirit.

Now Qwilleran was sure that Polly had suggested Unit Two to the new man in town. She was always discovering "interesting" men: a Chicago architect, a Canadian professor, an antiques dealer from Ohio . . . and now it appeared to be an actor! Why were women so easily mesmerized by actors? His own mother had fallen for an actor in a traveling company, but that was not all bad.

Qwilleran had a strong desire for a large dish of ice cream, but in the kitchen there was an aroma of overripe bananas. He had not been observing the doctor's advice. There were three bananas in the bowl on the bar, a handcrafted ceramic from the local art center. When empty it looked "arty." With three brownish bananas in it, it looked like a garbage receptacle!

He dumped them and had a large dish of ice cream.

FIVE

On Sunday Qwilleran was a willing guest at an impromptu dinner party, the purpose of which was to empty the Rikers' refrigerator. Mildred Riker was the food editor of the *Moose County Something*; her husband, Arch, was editor in chief — and a longtime friend of the "Qwill Pen" columnist. The couple had made a sudden decision to close their house at the lake and return to winter quarters in Indian Village.

When Mildred called Qwilleran with the invitation, she said, "After Labor Day the cottagers start moving out, and the shoreline gets bleak. If you don't mind helping us clear out the refrigerator . . ."

"Always glad to be of assistance," he said quickly. "I'm very good at emptying refrigerators. How many courses do you think you can squeeze out of the old box?"

"Five, at least. I called Polly, but she's not available. I called the Comptons, too. Lyle is out of town, but Lisa will be here. She can tell us all about the rare books they've found among the ESP donations."

When Qwilleran arrived, the day was sunny enough and the breezes balmy enough to permit cocktails on the deck overlooking the lake. Arch was serving drinks.

He was comfortably middle-aged — and plump from too much good eating. Mildred was plump and pretty. Toulouse, the half-starved stray they had rescued, lounged on the top rail of the deck. Now he was plump, too.

"Where's your wandering husband?" Qwilleran asked Lisa.

"He had to leave this morning for a three-day seminar in Saint Paul."

Arch said, "I wish I had his job! He gets all these out-of-town trips, paid for by the county, and we never notice any improvement in the school system. Makes you wonder what they do in Saint Paul."

"May I quote you?" she asked sweetly.

Qwilleran found Lisa friendly but authoritative, like a school principal on vacation. She dyed her hair. Lyle was a humorous grouch who was having a hard time saving his. When anyone asked them about their home life, Lisa would say, "We have a lot of fun. I don't let him get away with anything."

Qwilleran said, "Too bad Lyle can't be here today; I had planned to honor him with a limerick." He handed Lisa an index card with the following lines:

A school superintendent named Lyle
Runs the Moose County system with style.
He teaches teachers to teach,
And he makes a good speech,
But his disposition is vile.

His wife screamed, "He'll love it! He'll have it framed for his office!"

Arch complained, "How come no one ever writes a limerick about me?"

"I tried," Qwilleran said. "I've been trying for years! But you're not a hiker or a biker, and the only other rhyme for Riker is piker."

Now, Qwilleran asked, "Does anyone know the Bill Turmeric who writes witty letters to the 'Vox Pop' page?"

"Lyle knows him," Lisa said. "He teaches English in the Sawdust City system."

Mildred said, "He recently maintained that 'Go!' is the shortest sentence in the English language."

Qwilleran objected. "In our family, 'No!' is equally short and to the point. The problem is, no one pays any attention."

Then Mildred told Lisa she looked wonderful since volunteering for the ESP.

"Thank you. I'm so inspired by the challenge, I feel rejuvenated . . . especially when we find we've been given books worth as much as five thousand dollars."

"How did you discover them?"

"The K Fund put us in touch with a rare-book dealer in Chicago, who told us what to look for, like: important author, first edition, autographed, and, of course, good condition. We sent him a list of candidates, and he appraised them. Several are worth five hundred dollars, and a few are worth much more."

Arch said, "You'd never get me to pay five hundred for a book!"

"But hon," his wife protested, "you paid that much for a rusty piece of old tin!"

"That was a primitive piece of folk art with a provenance, and it was an auction for a good cause!"

Qwilleran said, "ESP promotes literacy, and that's a good cause." Then he added slyly, "The more people who learn to read in Moose County, the more newspapers you sell!"

"I need another drink," Arch said. "Who's ready?"

"Hon, I'm about to serve now," Mildred said. "Would you open the wine and feed Toulouse?"

Dinner began with a mysterious soup, followed by a mysterious casserole and another unidentified course called a savory. The dessert was equally mysterious, but everything tasted good.

During the meal they discussed the new play, the two actors from Lockmaster who were so good, and the possibility that the show might run for three weekends — a local record.

Then Qwilleran asked, "Has anyone heard that Alden Wade is taking a condo in Indian Village?"

"I doubt it," said Lisa. "He's been living at the Hibbard Guest House and is enthusiastic about it. Violet Hibbard is on the ESP board of directors, you know."

Mildred said, "I knew her in grade school. She was always serious, being an only child and accustomed to being with adults. She was an all-A student and made the rest of us look bad, so we were glad when she was sent to a private school in the East."

"She's still serious," Lisa said, "but she's developed a kind of warm feeling for people. Maggie Sprenkle, her only longtime friend, says that Violet taught at an American university in Italy for a while, early in her career, and when she came home, she was a different person."

"It's those Italian men!" Arch said.

"Oh, hon!" his wife protested.

Qwilleran asked, "Did she never marry?"

"No, and she's the last of the Hibbards," Lisa said. "They were never a large family, and the flu epidemic of 1918 wiped out almost a whole generation, according to Maggie."

"This is off the record, of course, but she donated most of the books that turned out to be rare."

Arch asked, "Can she take her donations as a tax deduction?"

"I believe so."

"Do you have a record of who gave what?"

"Yes. The information is in the computer but not for publication."

Mildred said, "This is all so interesting!"

Lisa went on, "Faulkner, Hemingway, Virginia Woolf, T. S. Eliot, Raymond Chandler, and Dr. Seuss are among the valuable books we have. . . . Strange to say, the Dr. Seuss books seldom show up in the rare-book market. Is that because they don't survive family wear and tear? But we have *The Cat in the Hat* that didn't get chewed by a dog."

"I'll take it!" Qwilleran said. "Koko will sit on it to keep it warm. He knows a significant book when he smells one."

Arch said, "I hope all these valuable books are going to be kept in a safe."

"We'll keep them under lock and key," Lisa said, "and show potential customers an inventory of what's available. And that brings up another thing: Violet spotted a wonderful antique jelly cupboard at Susan Exbridge's shop. It's priced at three thousand, but she'll give it to us for half price."

Arch asked, "What does a jelly cupboard have to do with books? If it isn't too dumb a question."

Lisa explained, "Families used to keep their home-canned goods locked in a cabinet. Don't ask me why. Susan's so-called jelly cupboard is big enough to hold over a hundred books in upper and lower sections. Both sections have locks."

Mildred said, "I've seen that in her shop! It's a handsome pine piece — elegant in its simplicity."

"Exactly!" Lisa said. "It would be the focal point of the ESP shop."

Arch said, "How come she's selling it for half price? She should give it to you for

60

nothing. If you're afraid to ask her for it, send Qwill to twist her arm!"

"I second the motion," Lisa said.

"I make it unanimous!" Mildred cried. "He's good at twisting arms."

Qwilleran huffed into his moustache. "How soon do you need it?"

"Not later than Wednesday," Lisa said. "One of our volunteers has a van, and he'll pick it up."

Arch asked, "Who's for an after-dinner drink?"

Qwilleran said he had to go home and feed the cats before they started chewing the rugs. Lisa wanted to get home before dark. The Compton beach house was a quarter mile down the shore, and she had walked over.

Qwilleran was only too happy to drive her home; he had a question to ask: "Have you met Alden Wade? He has a strong presence onstage; what is he like as a person?"

"He's charming!" she said. "And so helpful! Although he's hired to do specific things for the bookstore, he comes downstairs to ask if he can do anything for the ESP. And that's not all! A couple of weeks ago he brought me a long-stemmed red rose in a bud vase and told me to watch it open day by day. He said it's inspirational! . . . Then I found out that he gave Polly one! And also Violet, his landlady! I think that was very sweet of him, and it makes me think he's lonely."

Or he's covering all the bases, Qwilleran thought. Then he wondered why Polly had not mentioned the rose during one of their nightly phone chats. And he speculated about the rumor that Alden Wade was buying Unit Two. Perhaps he had looked at it just to please Polly. Perhaps she had suggested it!

"Well, thanks for the lift, Qwill," Lisa said, "and while you're here, let me give you a copy of our rare-book list. Tell me if you want to buy the Dr. Seuss for Koko."

He drove home and found two hungry cats looking aggrieved because their dinner was late.

"Sorry!" he said. "But wait till you see what Mildred has sent you!"

The square plastic box contained not only the leftover casserole for the Siamese but a few items for human consumption: cookies, dinner rolls, apples, and two bananas past their prime.

Qwilleran divided the mysterious casserole between the two dishes under the kitchen table and stood by to observe their rapturous gobbling. Instead, they sniffed their plates and walked away, flicking their tails in irritation.

"Please!" Qwilleran protested. "You're entitled to your opinion, but this is going too far!"

He knew they would gobble Mildred's delicacies as soon as his back was turned.

Later that evening Qwilleran sprawled in his favorite thinking chair and considered Susan Exbridge, the individual whose arm he was expected to twist.

He jerked to attention for a moment as he heard Koko's gut-wrenching howl that had come to be known as his "death howl." More likely, he decided, it was evidence of catly indigestion following the mysterious casserole.

Susan Exbridge was a character, no doubt about it! She amused him with her pretensions and affectations, and he enjoyed teasing her and scolding her occasionally. He could get away with it because of his connection with the K Fund.

Susan had a great respect for money. In Pickax she was considered a snob. She received a goodly amount of alimony, bought her clothes in Chicago, and drove a status car. Her shop, Exbridge & Cobb Fine Antiques, was so high-toned that locals were afraid to enter — except to hurry to the annex, where the primitives were kept, huddled together like poor relations. They were the collection of the late Iris Cobb, who had left them to her partner. Mrs. Cobb's extensive library of books on antiques now filled the shelves in Susan's office, although Polly said Mrs. Exbridge had never read a book in her life. There was a slight clash of personalities here, no doubt exacerbated by Susan's custom of greeting Qwilleran with an effusive "dahling."

Now he had to convince her to donate the jelly cupboard to a good cause. The K Fund could contribute it easily, but the idea was to teach Susan a lesson in community involvement.

The easy way would be to storm into her shop and say, "Susan! I hear you're selling Mrs. Cobb's jelly cupboard to the ESP! Isn't that rather shoddy business? After all, it was Mrs. Cobb's, and you didn't pay a penny for it! Your rich friends are donating five-thousand-dollar books! Surely you could manage a three-thousand-dollar jelly cupboard. . . . You know, you can take it as a tax deduction."

A confrontation would be easy and effective but too obvious. He would prefer something more subtle, even devious.

Then he thought of the Moose County method of making things happen: Spread the rumor and, before anyone knows, it's a fact.

He phoned Polly Duncan. First he listened patiently to the details of organizing her winter wardrobe. Then he described the impromptu dinner she had missed, adding, "And by the way, I heard some surprising news! Susan Exbridge is donating a three-thousand-dollar cabinet to the ESP!"

"I can't believe it!" Polly cried. "She never gives anything away! And she always referred to Eddington as 'that dreadful little man.' How do you explain it, Qwill?"

"Hard to say. You might check it out with some of your sources. It's certainly good news — if it's true."

"I'll make a few calls right away. Hang up, dear! Thanks for letting me know. . . . À bientôt!"

"À bientôt."

Qwilleran hung up with satisfaction. In the morning he would visit Susan's shop and congratulate her.

Having plotted the jelly cupboard

strategy to his satisfaction, he tuned in WPKX and heard a bulletin that snapped him to attention: a fatal car accident at the Black Creek bridge at eight-fifteen p.m. That was the precise moment that Koko had uttered his ominous howl. It had nothing to do with feline indigestion: It was Koko's death howl. Qwilleran had heard it many times before. It always signified wrongful death. The victim's name was not released in the bulletin.

SIX

 It was early Monday morning. Qwilleran was groggily pressing the button on his automated coffeemaker. The cats were staggering down the ramp from their sleeping quarters on the third balcony — stretching, yawning, waking up their fur with electrifying shudders.

He had forgotten about the WPKX news bulletin until Carol Lanspeak phoned. "Qwill! Did you hear about the accident last night? The victim's name has just been released! It was Ronnie. It was our Ronnie! You know — Ronald Dickson, who played Algernon! I feel terrible about it — such a nice young man — and he was going to be married soon."

"Sad news," Qwilleran murmured. "What were the circumstances? Does anyone know?"

"A few members of the cast went to Onoosh's to celebrate after the matinee. Ronnie had to drive back to Lockmaster. He missed the curve at the bridge. We're canceling all performances and refunding ticket money. Will your review be running today — anyway?"

"On the entertainment page, but call the city desk immediately and request a front-page bulletin: all performances canceled owing to the death of a member of the cast. And when I file my copy this morning, I'll check to see that the bulletin gets a prominent position."

When domestic matters at the barn were resolved to the satisfaction of all concerned, Qwilleran drove to the office of the *Something* to file his review of the play. Walking down the long corridor to the managing editor's office, he said "Hi!" to a young man hurrying in the opposite direction with a fistful of proofs — the new copyboy, apparently. Only copyboys hurried. This one had a beard, and longer hair than was usual.

"New copyboy?" Qwilleran said to Junior Goodwinter.

"Copy facilitator," Junior corrected him.

"Isn't he rather hirsute?"

"Times have changed since you hacked for a living. . . . Is that your review of the play?"

Qwilleran handed him his copy. "Did you and Jody see the production?"

"Sunday afternoon. We thought it was great! Rotten news about the fatal accident. We're running a bulletin in a black border on the front page. Obit tomorrow. Who's the best source of information?"

"Wetherby Goode at WPKX and Alden Wade at the bookstore."

"And what's the topic for tomorrow's 'Qwill Pen'?"

"A brief history of literacy in Moose County — leading into community involvement in the ESP."

Junior said, "This is a big week for Moose County! Dwight Somers guarantees we'll get national coverage. Roger, Bushy, and Jill will cover the press preview for us and we'll give it the front page and picture page on Friday."

Qwilleran said, "They'd better have the mounted sheriff's corps on the scene for the public opening Saturday. Hundreds turned out for the groundbreaking; how many thousands will show up for the public opening?"

Qwilleran waited until he knew the antiques shop would be open and then blustered into Susan's front door in excitement.

She was talking to two customers and

looked up in surprise. "Dahling! What brings you here in such a jovial mood?"

"I came to congratulate you, Susan, on your generosity in donating the jelly cupboard to ESP in memory of Eddington Smith!"

"Where did you hear that?" she asked cagily.

"It's all over town! There are no secrets in our fair city."

Even if she had wanted to deny it, the presence of two customers made it impossible. Actually, the scenario could not have been more cleverly staged.

"Someone will be here to pick it up before Thursday, which is when the out-of-town media will be here. May I look at it — in case I have a chance to describe it in the 'Qwill Pen'?"

Susan helplessly waved him toward the annex and followed him there, saying only a weak "excuse me" to the customers.

Qwilleran said, "Handsome finish on the pine. How would I describe it?"

With only slight hesitation, she said, "The patina of age — and loving care."

"Does it have a provenance?"

"It belonged to an old family on Purple Point."

The fabrication amused Qwilleran, who

had seen the cupboard in Iris Cobb's apartment — in Junktown, Down Below.

He said, "A volunteer from ESP will be here to pick it up. He'll call first."

Qwilleran had yet another mission to perform downtown. Once a week he did Polly's grocery shopping, putting the purchases in the trunk of her car, with the perishables in a cooler. Under ordinary circumstances he would then be invited to a home-cooked dinner of last week's leftovers. There had been no ordinary circumstances, however, since Polly undertook the challenge of running a bookstore. He was keeping score, of course, and she now owed him twenty dinners.

He always took her list to Toodle's Market, and Grandma Toodle always assisted him in selecting the fruits and vegetables. He might buy some Delicious apples for himself as well, and lately he was buying bananas. On this occasion he complained to Grandma Toodle that the bananas always turned brown before they could be eaten.

"How many in your family?" she asked.

"Three, but only one of us eats bananas."

"Then don't buy so many at once," she

advised, "and be sure they don't have any brown spots."

He selected four and was about to push his cart away, when he found it blocked by another piled high with cornflakes, flour, cat litter, sacks of potatoes, and gallons of milk. The shopper was a rosy-cheeked woman with the air of a happy housewife.

"Mr. Q," she said, recognizing his moustache, "what you need is a banana hook."

"I didn't know there was such a thing," he replied.

"All you need is an old-fashioned wire coat hook — the kind you see everywhere. Just screw it into the side of a wooden kitchen cupboard and hang up the bananas. Don't put them in a bowl or on a counter."

He thanked her graciously and wondered if he could write a thousand words for the "Qwill Pen" on the importance of having a banana hook. He would take a humorous approach. Bananas are funny; apples and oranges are not. There was something humorous about slipping on a banana peel, according to the old comic strips.

At home, Qwilleran found a clothes hook in the broom closet and screwed it into a wood surface in the kitchen. Problem solved! . . . or so he thought.

★ ★ ★

That evening, Qwilleran set out to con himself into eating a banana. He recalled his boyhood pleasure in clutching a banana like an ice-cream cone and peeling it down a little at a time. He recalled his boyhood dream of a banana split — never realized because his mother said it was too expensive. Thus fortified psychologically, he unhooked a banana and had just finished peeling it at the kitchen counter when the phone rang. He placed the naked fruit on a strip of peel and answered after the third ring. He thought it might be Polly, and he preferred to sit at the desk rather than stand at the kitchen phone.

It was not Polly. It was a woman's husky voice asking for Ralph.

"No one here by that name," he said. He should have hung up immediately, but . . . perhaps he was postponing the eating of the banana.

"Are you sure?" she asked.

"Quite!"

"Is this Wilson's Bar?"

"No, it is not Wilson's Bar. What number are you calling?"

She gave the number of the apple barn.

"You dialed correctly, but you've been given the wrong number. Who gave you

73

this number?" By this time, Qwilleran was enjoying the conversation. It was beginning to sound like a comedy act. Or it might be a practical joke, and he wondered which one of his friends could be guilty. Wetherby Goode was the only one he could summon to mind.

The woman was saying, "Ralph told me I could reach him at this number."

"Well, I'm afraid he lied to you, madam."

She slammed down the receiver, and Qwilleran chuckled. He was headed back to the kitchen when the phone rang again. This time he was sure it was Polly. "Good evening," he said in the ultra-friendly voice that amused her.

"Is Ralph there?" came the same husky voice.

This time Qwilleran slammed down the receiver, not in anger but in pleasant anticipation of telling the story to Polly — when she called.

The banana was waiting for him — but not the peel. Where was the peel? He was sure he had left it on the kitchen counter!

Then, out of the corner of his eye, he glimpsed something yellow on the floor. A strip of banana peel — with fang marks.

"You heathens!" he yelled. It was only a

quarter of a total peel. Where was the rest of it? It could be dangerous underfoot! First he inspected all the hard surfaces: floor, tile, and flagstone. The Siamese were of no help at all. Ordinarily they would join the search, sniffing and scratching, but they were hiding, in evident guilt.

He looked in the wastebaskets, where Yum Yum usually deposited her loot. No banana peel. He walked up the ramp (carefully) to the three balconies. If he could find the cats, he thought, he could find the peel.

The search was interrupted by Polly's call. "Am I calling too late?" she asked. "I just got home! We all had a wonderful time."

Preoccupied with his own problem, Qwilleran listened inattentively. The gist of it was this: Dwight Somers of Somers & Beard, local public relations firm, had been retained by the K Fund to handle publicity for The Pirate's Chest.

And prior to the press preview, Dwight had taken the entire staff to dinner at the Mackintosh Inn. That meant Polly, her assistant, three contingency aides in green smocks, and Alden Wade.

"We had a private dining room," she

went on. "Alden and Dwight kept up a nonsensical banter about Dundee, and the secret statue under cover in the park, rare books in the jelly cupboard, borrowing limousines from the funeral home to pick up the out-of-town press, and so forth.

"And what did you do today, dear?" Polly concluded.

"Nothing much," he said.

"Thank you so much for the groceries, dear."

"My pleasure. *À bientôt.*"

"*À bientôt.*"

The phone rang once more that evening, and a gruff male voice with a Scottish accent said, "Are you still serving drinks without a license?"

"Only to police chiefs. Come on over, Andy."

Qwilleran set out Scotch, ice cubes, Squunk water, glasses, and a platter of cheese and crackers on the snack bar, then went to the barnyard to meet his guest.

Andrew Brodie was a towering Scot with a menacing swagger whether wearing a police uniform or a bagpiper's kilt and bonnet. In mufti he still had an air of authority. The cats were waiting to greet him at the kitchen door. They knew that the big man with the loud voice always slipped them a morsel of cheddar or Gouda from the cheese platter.

Sitting at the snack bar, the two men poured their own drinks, and Andy said, "Still drinkin' Squunk water? You're gonna turn into a Squunk."

"Better than turning into a casualty at the Black Creek bridge," Qwilleran said. "Did Fran say anything about it?"

"Haven't seen her. M'wife and two other daughters saw the show. They said it was good."

"Do you know if Fran went out celebrating with the other actors after the matinee?"

"Nope."

Qwilleran said, "The fellow who was killed had been coming down from Lockmaster for rehearsals, and he should have known about the tricky curve at the bridge."

"They shouldn't bring in outsiders for the Pickax shows," Brodie said. "Y'never know what they're up to. The medical examiner said the driver was on drugs. Drugs and alcohol — that's murder! Larry and Carol don't allow no drugs in the club. Their youngest kid was on drugs when he ran his car into the side of a moving freight train."

"I'm shocked to hear about the medical report, Andy. I wonder if the Lanspeaks know?"

"They'll have a fit when they find out. . . . Say, this is good cheese!"

SEVEN

Qwilleran walked downtown to file his Tuesday "Qwill Pen" column before the noon deadline and returned by way of Granny's Sweet Shop. His recent ruminations about banana splits had given him the urge to try one for lunch. He reasoned that it would provide his banana for the day. And he was in a good mood when he returned to the apple barn in time to hear the phone ringing.

A man's voice said, "Mr. Qwilleran? Mrs. Duncan gave me your phone number."

"Don't tell me! Let me guess! You're Jack Worthing aka Ernest."

"You have a good ear, sir."

"You have a distinctive voice, sir. What can I do for you?"

"Mrs. Duncan has assigned me to start a literary club under the auspices of the bookstore, and she thinks you will have some input. Could you spare some time this afternoon?"

"Gladly! At the store? Or here?"

"With only two days to go before the press preview, things are a little hectic over here —"

"Then come to the barn. Do you know where it is?"

"Behind the theatre and through the woods?"

"Are you in the mood for coffee or a cold drink?"

"I think I'd like to try your infamous coffee."

Without ever having met the man, Qwilleran liked the timbre of his voice and his economy with words. A few minutes later they were shaking hands in the barnyard and exchanging first names.

Alden gazed up at the lofty octagonal building. "This is beyond my wildest imaginings, Qwill. And you live here alone?"

"No, I live with two Siamese cats, who are the equivalent of a large family." Glancing at his visitor's briefcase, he added, "Shall we sit at the conference table?"

Papers were spread out and coffee was served at the dining table, hardly ever used for anything but small meetings and large cocktail parties, such as the famous cheese-tasting at which Koko went bananas and literally trashed the whole scene. The black-tie crowd who had paid three hundred dollars a ticket — for charity — never forgot it.

Alden said, "We have a list here of fifty persons who have shown an interest in a lit club, patterned after the one in Lock-master."

Glancing at the list, Qwilleran saw the names of the school superintendent, the president of the community college, two attorneys, doctors, retired academics, a professional astrologer, and artists. "What kind of programming do you propose?"

"Book reviews, lectures, discussions of preassigned books. The names on this list will be invited to attend a planning session. At this meeting everyone would like you to be our first speaker."

"Hmmm . . ." Qwilleran mused. "Any suggested topic?"

"How about a profile of Eddington Smith, since you probably knew him better than any other customer."

"How many hours can I have?" Qwilleran asked.

That settled, they went on to talk of other matters.

About Mrs. Duncan, as he called her with unnecessary formality: "A charming woman. Cultivated voice. Good executive."

About Ronald Dickson: "Sad! Very sad! He had his theatre training in my class at the academy. He was a natural when it came to acting, but he lacked confidence. He thought popping pills would solve the problem. Not true! I don't approve of amphetamines. There are techniques to be learned. But he wanted shortcuts. Poor Ronnie."

Qwilleran said to his guest, "Have you found a satisfactory place to live?"

"The Hibbard House. Excellent accommodations. A good cook. Charming hostess. Congenial guests. One can always find four for bridge or a party for duck hunting. There's a good library . . . and a music room with a Steinway."

"Any pets?" Qwilleran asked.

"No personal pets. But Violet has a watchdog named Tasso that has won me over. In fact, I've asked her permission to take full responsibility for him. I've always had at least two dogs, and I miss them."

"I know how you feel," Qwilleran said, thinking about Koko and Yum Yum.

"There's one strict rule. No smoking on the premises — anywhere. The house is over a hundred years old and built completely of wood. There are fire extinguishers everywhere, some disguised as art objects."

Qwilleran said, "About the dog: Where does he hang out in this magnificent place?"

"He has a separate room, just off the kitchen, and his own screened porch. He's an Italian breed, a Bracco, and one of the best gun dogs I've ever hunted with. You must come with us some weekend."

"How did you find this choice place, Alden?"

"Violet Hibbard is on the ESP board, and Mrs. Compton introduced us." There was much sympathy for the widower, and he happened to be a good-looking man with polished manners. It was common knowledge that there was a waiting list for accommodations. Lisa had apparently pulled strings.

By the time the polished guest left, he had lined up the first speaker for the literary club.

Only then did Qwilleran realize that the Siamese had not made an appearance while Alden was on the premises. Did they sense he was a dog person? Now they were walking with the stiff-legged gait and stiffened tails that denoted disapproval.

And yet the Siamese always welcomed Culvert McBee, the farmboy who lived on the back road, and he always had dogs. He sheltered old, unwanted dogs in a shed on the family farm, a hobby that his parents encouraged. So did Qwilleran, who maintained a Koko Fund to cover veterinary expenses. To raise money for dog food, Culvert sold small handcrafted items, his mother's cookies, and fruit from their ancient pear tree, said to be older than Pickax. Pears ranked next to bananas on Qwilleran's least-favored-fruit list, but they were welcomed by fellow staffers at the *Something*.

So it was not Alden Wade's canine connection that turned off the Siamese. Was he wearing a scent discernible only to a cat's sensitive nose? Did his lofty mode of speech offend their delicate ears? Yum Yum had not even made her usual stealthy search for something small and shiny to steal. Qwilleran's puzzlement only increased his curiosity about the new man in town.

Altogether it was a busy afternoon at the apple barn: First, Alden Wade with stimulating news about the Hibbard House . . . then Culvert with another bag of

84

pears . . . and finally Dwight Somers with news about Thursday's press preview at The Pirate's Chest. The publicist from Down Below had a knack for dramatizing events in the boondocks.

"Glass of wine?" Qwilleran offered him.

"Not this time, thanks. I have work to do tonight. But I'll try a glass of that stuff you drink."

They sat at the snack bar with Squunk water on the rocks, with a twist, and Dwight pulled papers from his briefcase: press releases for four separate news events.

Dwight said, "I'll give you a quick rundown. TV and print media will arrive by chartered planes from four major cities; they like to report on bizarre happenings in remote areas. They'll be met at the airport by limousines, and we'll make sure they know they're borrowed from the Dingleberry Funeral Home.

"The major event will be the ribbon cutting, with Mayor Amanda Goodwinter wearing her usual scarecrow clothing and putting on her usual bad-tempered act. There's nothing diplomatic about Amanda. She says ribbon cutting is stupid and she'll have none of it. The president of the city council will be there, and the fact

85

that Scott Gippel weighs three hundred pounds won't hurt a bit. Your attorney will represent the K Fund, and Polly will represent the bookstore.

"They may or may not want Polly to hold the bibliocat. In any case, Dundee is going to steal the show. He's fearless, inquisitive, and persistent.

"Indoors, the pirate's chest up on the wall will make a good shot, with people on the staircase looking up at it. The history of it will be covered in the releases."

Dwight stopped for a slug of Squunk water and said, "Hey! This isn't bad! Refreshing!" Then he continued. "Next, the Edd Smith Place. It's unusual for a commercial bookstore to give a third of the building to pre-owned books, with proceeds going to charity. Hundreds of books have been donated, including some rare titles worth as much as five thousand. The releases will cover the quaint feldspar building that stood on the site for a century and a half until destroyed by an arsonist. Mention is made of Winston Churchill, the bibliocat who dusted the dusty old books with his plumed tail and miraculously escaped the fire.

"And that leads up to the final story: Winston Park — a walk-and-learn park with paths meandering among two dozen evergreens of the pine, spruce, cedar, hemlock, and holly families — all suitable for our northern climate. The focal point of the park is the mystery statue that will be unveiled for the cameras."

Qwilleran said, "It makes me wish I were a reporter covering the story for *The Daily Fluxion* or *Morning Rampage*. How long will it take the crews to cover all the angles? And what about the ever-hungry press?"

"Glad you asked, Qwill. Lunch will be served in one of the public rooms of the bookstore, where there are tables and chairs. Lois's Luncheonette will cater, with Lois herself joshing and bullying the media as she slices a turkey and a roast of beef and makes sandwiches on *real bread*. Her son, Lenny, will serve the apple pie and coffee. . . . Do you think we have a story, Qwill?"

When Qwilleran talked to Polly on the phone that evening, he said, "Dwight Somers dropped in to give me a rundown on the press preview. He's a real pro! He told me everything except what's hidden under the tarpaulin in the park."

"That's because he doesn't know. I

know, but I'm not going to tell you," she said with evident satisfaction, knowing that he deplored unanswered questions.

"And what did you do today that's not top secret?"

"Everyone's been guessing about the statue. The consensus is that it's a space capsule. . . . But wait till you hear about the decision I made today! I've created another position, assistant to Dundee! You see, one of our Green Smocks — Peggy, who's moving into the Winston Park apartments — offered to come in seven days a week to take care of Dundee's needs. Suddenly it occurred to me that *someone* has to buy cat food and litter and police his commode and feed him twice a day. Why not assign one of the Green Smocks to that responsibility?"

"Is she completely reliable?"

"Definitely! And she adores Dundee. What do you think of it, Qwill?"

"I'd like to apply for the position of assistant to Dundee's assistant. What does it pay?"

EIGHT

Grudgingly, Qwilleran chomped his bowl of cereal and sliced bananas that morning, instead of the sweet, sticky bachelor breakfast that had formerly ushered in his days. He wondered whether he would experience any increased productivity or brilliant ideas or improved writing skills. He doubted it . . . although an idea struck him while chomping, and he considered its possibilities. He had recently written three books — a collection of local legends, a compilation of cat lore, and the text for a portfolio of Moose County photographs — all published by the K Fund. Now, how about . . . ?

He phoned the county historian at home. "Thorn, what do you know about the Hibbard Guest House?"

"I don't know what it is now, but I know what it used to be. The Hibbards are one of those four-generation pioneer families, you know. Old fellow who built the house was illiterate but rich; his great-granddaughter is a professor of literature and, I presume, well off."

"What do you know about the house he built?"

"He was an eccentric duck. He built the largest house — on the highest hill in the county — in the most unusual style, and he built it entirely of wood. He owned saw-mills. The amazing thing is that it's still standing! Why do you ask?"

"Do you think it would make a good book for the K Fund to publish?"

"I'm sure it's full of ghosts, if you can interview them. And as an example of nineteenth-century architecture, it's certainly unique."

The historian had said the magic word; in Qwilleran's vocabulary, "unique" meant newsworthy.

Qwilleran said to him, "It seems to me, Thorn, that you're one of those fourth-generation families — going on fifth."

"Yeah, we've been thinking about rounding them all up for the Pickax sesquicentennial. But when we've got them rounded up, what do we do with them?"

"Good question," Qwilleran agreed.

Upon returning to the kitchen to rinse his cereal bowl and tidy the counter, Qwilleran realized he had forgotten to put the banana peel under lock and key. Before he could go looking for it, the phone rang.

"Yes?" he barked into the mouthpiece.

"Qwill! You sound mad as a hornet! Want me to call back? This is Lisa."

"Sorry. That's what bananas do to me. I called earlier to see if Violet Hibbard will be in today."

"From two o'clock on. She's dying to meet you, Qwill."

Both cats were probably guilty of the banana-peel misdemeanor; they failed to respond when he announced, "Your uncle George is coming!" The attorney was coming for another shot in the arm.

At the dining table, Allen Barter opened his briefcase and reported on the Winston Park apartments, a property of the K Fund. All units had been rented, and tenants were moving in.

When it was Qwilleran's turn to report, he broached the idea of a book on the historic Hibbard House, said to be unique. "It's one of the oldest houses in the county. The K Fund should publish it before it burns down."

"Is that the big house on the hill?" the attorney asked. "I pass the gate on my way downtown."

"It's one of those four-generation families. I'm meeting with the last remaining Hibbard this afternoon. She's a retired professor; her great-grandfather — who amassed the fortune and built the house — was illiterate. I have yet to see the house, but I'm sure there are plenty of photo possibilities for John Bushland, and enough folktales to make a good text."

"The Big Boys in Chicago are pleased with the sales of your other three titles," Bart said. "I'm sure they'll welcome another."

When Qwilleran arrived at the Edd Smith Place, volunteers in green vests were bustling about and Dundee was investigating the computer. A woman in a tailored black pantsuit came forward with hand outstretched. "I'm Violet Hibbard, and you're the redoubtable Mr. Q."

He took her hand, bending over it slightly in the courtly way he had with women of a certain age. "I've always wanted to meet someone called Violet! Are you prepared to tell all?"

"I'm looking forward to it. Shall we repair to one of the meeting rooms?"

Qwilleran liked her vocabulary and her personality — not overly friendly, and not suspiciously charming, but . . . vibrant and intelligent. As they walked down the hall, Qwilleran detected a light scent that was probably violet. They sat in one of the meeting rooms.

For openers he said, "There is talk about publishing a book on the Hibbard House as a historic masterpiece in Moose County."

"It would please me greatly, and you're the only one I'd trust to write it, Mr. Q."

"Please call me Qwill, because I'm going to call you Violet."

"Then may I ask you a question? Have you ever acted on the stage? I recognize a certain quality in your voice and in your bearing that suggests a theatre background."

Pleased by the compliment but wanting to keep the conversation light, he replied, "In high school I was the youngest King Lear in the annals of Shakespeare. Miraculously, no one laughed at the gray beard."

"That's because you were sincere. Did you ever act professionally?"

"No. I did a few plays in college but then switched to journalism. Recently, though, I learned something that indicates I have acting in my genes. My father, who died before I was born, was an actor with a road company playing in Chicago when my mother met him. He had the lead in what she called a dismal Russian play."

"No doubt it was *The Lower Depths*, Gorky's best play and the only one that would be playing in the U.S. at that time."

"Is that so?" he said in surprise. "Then listen to this. Twenty years later, I was in college and playing the role of Satine, the philosophical crook in *The Lower Depths*! In the last act he has a long, highly dramatic scene. While I was intoning the lines with vehemence and strong gestures, I had a sudden feeling of déjà vu that gave me goose bumps! Only recently did I see some of my mother's correspondence at the time, in which she mentioned the Russian play!"

"Do you remember any of your lines?"

"A few." He thought a moment, stood up, and then proclaimed in what he called his Carnegie Hall voice:

"Shut up, you fools! You lie like the Devil! You're all as dumb as stones! . . . I know what lying means. The weakling — and whoever is a parasite to his own weakness — they both need lies. But the man who is free, who is strong — he needs no lies. Truth is the religion of the free man . . . and why can't a crook speak the truth, since honest people at times speak like crooks."

Qwilleran looked at his hands as if remembering how he had used them in his argument.

Violet cried, "Bravo! I felt a tremor of emotion myself!"

Dundee came running to see what was happening.

"Do you have a special interest in drama?" Qwilleran asked.

"Drama and poetry — the two subjects that were my specialty." Then with a roguish glance she added, "Have you played any Shakespeare since *King Lear*?" She asked it with a twinkle in her eyes, which Qwilleran suddenly realized were violet. Was it natural? Could it be done with contact lenses? Didn't Elizabeth Taylor have violet eyes? Yum Yum's blue eyes had a violet tint.

Snapping out of his pondering, he replied, "In college I played Brutus in *Julius Caesar* and Bottom in *Midsummer Night's Dream*. Most recently I was rehearsing with the Pickax Theatre Club for *Arsenic and Old Lace*. I was the crazy brother. Unfortunately, it never opened, but that's a long story."

"With your Teddy Roosevelt moustache, you were well cast. Did you ever do any Mark Twain readings?"

Obviously they had much to talk about, and Qwilleran said, "I think we should have dinner some evening. We haven't begun to discuss Molière, Ibsen, and Euripides. I could suggest the Old Grist Mill Friday night."

"I'd be delighted!" she cried, her eyes flashing violet again.

Later he phoned the restaurant. "I'd like to reserve a table for two. This is Jim Qwilleran."

"Hi, Mr. Q! This is Derek. It's been a long time since we saw you and Mrs. Duncan."

"I'm not taking Mrs. Duncan, Derek, so watch your step!"

"Oh-oh! I put my foot in my mouth again. Sorry! . . . Do you have a choice of table, Mr. Q?"

Amiably, Qwilleran said, "The one beneath the scythe, if it's available." The restaurant walls were decorated with old-time farm implements. "Just be sure it's firmly attached to the wall."

Qwilleran chuckled over Derek's innocent faux pas as he prepared dinner for the Siamese. They sat tall, shoulder to shoulder, waiting. What was going through

96

their little brown heads? he wondered. He had run out of homilies to inspire them and witticisms to entertain them. He paraphrased a little Shakespeare: *To be fed, or not to be fed, that is the question.* They flicked neither an ear nor a whisker. All they wanted was their food.

"Okay, you ungrateful brats. I'm going to dinner at Lois's, and I may or may not bring you a treat. Today's special is meat loaf." Qwilleran knew very well why he talked to the cats. It was to hear the sound of a human voice in the cavernous emptiness of the barn.

He put on his owl-proof orange baseball cap and carried a flashlight: The days were getting shorter. He went by way of Walnut Street in order to check the readiness of the park.

The shrouded statue stood calmly, waiting for the next day's unveiling and Friday's "Qwill Pen" column, which would list the public's guesses as to its design. Some guesses made sense; some were ludicrous, good for a laugh; some were unprintable. The mysterious obelisk stood waiting in a kind of form-fitting canvas bag that had been dropped over it. To remove it, a grappling hook or a mechanical claw might be lowered from a helicopter, lifting the shroud and carrying it away, leaving onlookers on the ground to *ooh* and *aah!* It was an unlikely premise but not impossible. Qwilleran had learned that anything can happen in Pickax.

A male voice behind him said, "Hi, Mr. Q. Got it figured out?" It was the bearded copy facilitator from the newspaper.

"I was just wondering how they plan to unveil it. There isn't enough width on the paths to accommodate a derrick. . . . All I can say is: It had better be something good under that shroud, or the public will riot. . . . How do you like your new job?"

"I like it! Everybody's very friendly."

"I'm afraid I don't know your name."

"Kenneth. In the city room they call me Whiskers," he said with a grin.

"Is that so?" Qwilleran replied seriously. "I have a cat by that name. Very intelligent animal. That's because he has sixty whiskers instead of the usual forty-eight."

The copyboy looked skeptical and changed the subject abruptly. "Mr. Q, could I ask you a big favor?"

"Of course! But I reserve the right to refuse if it's illegal or hazardous to the health."

"I have one of your books. Would you sign it for me?"

"If I wrote it, I'll sign it. Which one do you have?" Qwilleran had recently written a collection of local legends, the text for a book of Moose County photographs, and a think-piece on life with Koko and Yum Yum.

So he was stunned when Ken said that he owned *City of Brotherly Crime*.

"What? . . . Where? . . . How?"

"I got it somewhere in Ohio. A public library was having a book sale."

"Amazing! It's been out of print for twenty years. I have a copy that Edd Smith found for me after a long search."

"It must be valuable," Ken said, "although I didn't pay much for it. It's in my luggage. I haven't unpacked everything yet. I just moved into one of these apartments."

"Then take it to the paper Friday morning, and I'll be happy to sign it when I file the copy for my column."

Happier, he thought, than anyone would understand. He had never dreamed that he would be asked to sign the long-forgotten and totally unmourned tome. He had written it while working in Philadelphia, and it had made him no friends.

 Then Qwilleran had meat loaf and mashed potatoes at Lois's, where he heard gossip about couples who elope to Bixby County, a county noted for quick marriage licenses and accommodating judges. Qwilleran walked home with a slight detour past the bookstore. Sure enough, Polly's car was the only one in the parking lot; she was working late again. He rang the doorbell at the side entrance.

Dusk was falling, and she opened the door cautiously. Then, "Qwill!" she cried. "What a pleasant surprise. Come in! Have a chair!"

"You're working late again," he said with a note of disapproval.

"There's so much to do: decisions to make, problems to solve," she explained. The gentle, musical voice he had always found spine-tingling was now flat and weary.

He said, "Hold out for three days more, Polly, and then we'll both be back to normal living. I've missed our dinner dates and evenings of music. What did you decide about keys?"

She brightened somewhat. "We've ordered five — one for you, since you're more or less the godfather of the store."

"I'm not sure I understand the title," he said. "Who gets the other four?"

"Key One is for me. I unlock the side

door and then open the front door for customers who will be waiting to get in — we hope. Key Two is for my assistant, who will have the same responsibilities on my day off. Key Three is for Dundee's assistant, who will have to come in twice a day, seven days a week, to feed him, put fresh water in his bowl, and attend to his facilities."

Qwilleran said, "That's a demanding assignment. I hope she's well paid."

"She's quite satisfied with the arrangement. She's moved into one of those apartments beyond the park and will be available for Green Smock duty if needed. You see, she has a computer and does programming out of her home. And then there's Key Four for Alden Wade, since many of the special events he manages will take place evenings."

When she stopped for breath, Qwilleran asked, "Will the ESP have a key?"

"Good question, Qwill. The ESP governing board agreed with me that the Edd Smith project is a charitable endeavor on the part of local citizens, and it has space in this building as a charitable gesture on the part of the bookstore. Therefore, it should observe bookstore hours, and the volunteers should come and go through the front door. Also, they should check in and out at the front desk and should park in the north parking lot."

"I presume the ESP door on the lower level will be locked when there are no volunteers on duty."

"Absolutely! And the shop's 'open' schedule will be posted on that door."

"Do they still have an army of volunteers?"

"The original 'army' has completed its task of collecting books and cataloging. Now Lisa has a smaller group of volunteers willing to mind the shop during certain hours. When they report for duty, they'll pick up the ESP key at the front desk and return it when they close. Lisa will schedule the volunteer shopkeepers, working from her home. There will be one or two a day — never more than three. You ask a lot of questions, Qwill. Are you planning to write something?"

"Not right away. I'm just curious." He stood up. "Now I'll let you get back to work."

"Not so fast!" Polly said. "Here's your key to the side door."

"*Hmmm,*" he mused. "Is it honorary? Or do I have responsibilities? If Dundee's assistant has a Sunday-morning hangover, will I be called to substitute?"

"Oh, Qwill! The thought never entered my mind, but now that you mention the subject . . . it's not a bad idea!"

NINE

 On Thursday morning the Siamese breakfasted grandly on Lois's meat loaf, while Qwilleran reluctantly sliced bananas into a bowl of dry cereal, wondering why he had found cereal exciting in his boyhood. He had grown up with the packaged variety, and the packaging itself had improved his reading skills. He could spell "ingredients" while other kids were learning to spell "cat" and "dog." Now, shopping at Toodle's Market, he had been overwhelmed by the enormous selection — until he spotted a famous slogan: Snap Crackle Pop! He bought two boxes, but the sound effects were somehow less intriguing to his middle-aged ears. He gift-wrapped the second box and dispatched it to Arch Riker's office by motorcycle messenger, anonymously.

Within minutes, the phone rang — more impatiently than usual, it seemed — and he purred a pleasant "good morning" into the mouthpiece.

"What's the matter with you?" came an

exasperated voice. "Are you cracking up?"

"Just a sentimental reminder of the good old days, Arch."

"*You* ate this stuff! I didn't eat this stuff! Mine had baseball cards in the box, and pictures of Niagara Falls."

"It's the spirit of the gesture that counts," Qwilleran said in a syrupy tone.

Arch growled into the phone, "If you haven't got anything better to do, get down here and help us put the paper to bed."

He slammed down the receiver, and Qwilleran went about his morning chores with satisfaction.

This was the day of the press preview, and Qwilleran attended the unveiling with his press card sticking out of his vest pocket and his orange baseball cap on his head. As he walked to Winston Park, sirens could be heard; the sheriff's patrol was escorting the visiting press from the airport.

Yellow tape roped off an area for news photographers and TV teams. At the center of the area was a mound of immense boulders that might have been left there by a prehistoric earthquake, interspersed with spiky holly shrubs. At its summit was a large cube of polished granite with WINSTON PARK chiseled on all four sides. This was the platform for the tall, cylindrical object about to be unveiled.

Although there had been no publicity about the event, a modest crowd had gathered outside the yellow tape. They had to step aside for a school bus when it delivered a load of passengers in black leotards and tights — the high-school acrobatic team plus two students with drums. The rumor was true that a derrick would lift the shroud, but it was a human derrick. The black-clothed figures positioned themselves among the boulders, forming a pyramid, at the apex of which was an agile figure with an oversized fishing reel. The drums began a slow, suspenseful roll. The shroud started to rise, revealing an irregular stack of books chiseled from granite and three times the normal size. The drumbeats quickened! More books appeared, piled one on top of another, making a pedestal for a sculpture: a bronze cat, twice life size, sitting tall in an attitude of superior intellect, while his plumed tail draped casually over the column of books.

"Winston!" shouted the onlookers amid cheers and applause.

Qwilleran thought, If only Edd Smith could see this!

The next scheduled event was the official ribbon cutting, and he stayed to watch — but only because it would please Polly if he was there. Later he would describe it in his personal journal.

Qwilleran left the dedication ceremonies in the same way he had arrived — on foot — waving to the motorists who looked at him and pedestrians who said, "Hi, Mr. Q!"

Arriving in the barnyard, he waved at the two Siamese, who waited for him in the kitchen window with ears pricked and tails stiffened into question marks. According to Qwilleran's watch, the performance was less of an affectionate welcome and more of a reminder that their noon snack was ten minutes late. Even before hanging up his orange hat and car keys, he prepared two plates of Kabbibbles, each with a tiny morsel of cheese buried like the prize in a box of Cracker Jack.

Then he carried a dish of ice cream up the ramp to his studio on the second balcony, where he worked on Friday's "Qwill Pen" column.

In the afternoon there was a phone call from Lisa Compton:

"Qwill! Good news. Edd Smith's Place is

getting its own telephone! We've been using an extension of the bookstore phone, and Burgess Campbell said that was bad business practice. He's going to pay the monthly phone bill. ESP will have its own listing in the telephone directory. Do you have a pencil handy? I'll give you the number."

"Who's handling the ESP story for the *Something*?" Qwilleran asked.

"Roger took the pictures, and Jill's writing the story. He got a wonderful shot of Dundee examining an Ernest Hemingway book worth five thousand."

"Did you tell Jill about the new phone?"

"We didn't know about it while they were here," Lisa said.

"Then call her at the paper and give her the number. Tell Jill: If a cat answers, callers will be advised to press one and leave a message."

"Oh, Qwill." She laughed. "Would they print that?"

"There's no harm in suggesting it; the readers like a laugh," Qwilleran said. "How did the shooting go?"

"They loved Dundee! He's such an extrovert. Dwight's release described him as 'official bibliocat' and said the Edd Smith Place sold pre-owned books priced anywhere from two dollars to five thousand. Naturally, the photographers wanted to see what a five-thousand-dollar book looks like. Alden Wade had volunteered to help us, so we put him in charge of the jelly cupboard. He had the keys hanging around his neck like a wine steward, and he kept an eagle eye on any rare book he took out of the cupboard."

"Don't forget I've spoken for the Dr. Seuss book," Qwilleran said.

The next call came from Wetherby Goode, who wanted to stop at the barn for a minute en route to the radio station.

When he arrived, Qwilleran asked, "Do you have time for a libation?"

"Well . . . just a nip."

They sat at the snack bar, attended by two chummy Siamese, who liked the weatherman.

Qwilleran asked, "What did you think of the unveiling?"

"They put on quite a show, didn't they? And the sculpture itself is a swell idea! I'm going to do a little tribute to Winston on my show tonight."

"He's still living, you know, Joe. He lives with the Bethunes on Pleasant Street.

What's the nature of your tribute?"

"Just a parody I wrote with apologies to my alma mater: 'Dear Old Winston! Dear Old Winston!' Be sure to tune in at eleven."

"I wouldn't miss it, Joe." Then Qwilleran asked, "Do you still go to Horseradish weekends?" The weatherman had been spending an inordinate amount of time in his hometown without explaining why.

"Not anymore! Things change!"

"Do you happen to know if they are talking about Ronnie's accident?"

"Yes, and they're in shock because of a nasty rumor that's circulating. People are whispering that it was caused by drugs and alcohol! His parents are crushed! And I'm furious! It can't be true!"

"It was in the medical examiner's report, Joe."

"Look here! I grew up with Ronnie, and he was always a health nut — eating the right food, taking vitamins, and never drinking anything stronger than a beer. You can't convince me those Lockmaster dudes could get him on drugs. Alden Wade called Ronnie's parents and offered sympathy. He couldn't believe the rumor either. . . . Did you know that Alden's from Horseradish?"

"All you talented people . . ." Qwilleran began.

"Yeah, there's something in the drinking water. But we all change our names when we go out into the real world. Alden was George; did you know that? He said that George is a good name for a political leader, but an actor needs a name with more sex appeal — like Alan, Alex, Alfie — names beginning with AL. He had his name legally changed to Alden Wade. And the gals have been swooning over him ever since."

Qwilleran asked, "How about you, Joe? Was yours legally changed to Wetherby Goode?"

"Nay, that's just a nickname. For a weather prognosticator, it's a lot better than Joe Bunker!"

"YOW!" was Koko's clarion comment.

Wetherby jumped up. "Gotta get to the station. . . . What's that on the floor?"

"Be careful!" Qwilleran picked it up. "Koko collects banana peels. Does Jet Stream have any interesting hobbies?"

While the dedication ceremonies were still fresh in his mind, Qwilleran expressed his sentiments on the pages of his personal journal.

111

Thursday, September 25 — I agree with Amanda Goodwinter: There must be a better way! To launch a seagoing vessel, a bottle of champagne is smashed on the hull. To dedicate a new building, ribbon is stretched across the façade, to be cut by a civic official, or a civic official's five-year-old daughter in a frilly dress.

Somehow — halfway between the champagne and the five yards of ribbon — there must be a sane compromise! . . . Anyway . . .

After the memorable unveiling of the Winston Park monument, the cameras turned to focus on the bookstore. Five yards of green ribbon were stretched across the glass doors and show windows of the building. Dwight Somers, swinging a large pair of shears, was jockeying the dignitaries into line. Polly and Bart, representing the K Fund, looked spiffy in a businesslike way. Burgess Campbell, on the board of the ESP, was striking in Highland attire: kilt, kneesocks, shoulder plaid, and cocky Glengarry bonnet. And, of course, he was accompanied by his guide dog, Alexander. Together they always steal the show when photographers are around.

But where were the two city officials? Dwight paced nervously and talked on a cell phone. Suddenly a police car drove up, and out stepped the pair representing City Hall. Her Honor, the mayor, had a golf hat jammed down on her straggly gray hair and looked as if she had been raking leaves on the City Hall lawn. The president of the Town Council — all three hundred pounds of him — was stuffed into a mechanic's greasy coveralls.

Dwight escorted them into the lineup and presented the shears.

"Not me!" Amanda growled. "No way!"

"I don't cut ribbons," Scott Gippel muttered.

Without a moment's hesitation the attorney stepped forward and said, in his courtroom voice, "It is traditional and appropriate for civic leaders to cut the ribbon as a gesture of welcome to a new business enterprise that will benefit the entire county." That guy Bart! He managed to mix authority with an ingratiating manner. Polly looked relieved. Alexander whimpered.

And Scott said, "Okay, gimme the

dang clippers and I'll cut the dang ribbon!"

I don't know how much of the dialogue was picked up by the mikes, but it resounded all over the park.

TEN

For the Siamese, it was a day like any other day; for the rest of the civilized population of Moose County, it was a breathless lull between the press preview and the public opening of the new bookstore. Qwilleran, being ahead of schedule with his writing, spent much of the morning brushing the cats' coats, entertaining them with a rollicking game of grab-the-necktie, and reading aloud to them from good literature. It was Koko's responsibility to select a title for reading and push it off the bookshelf. It was Qwilleran's responsibility to catch the book before it landed.

For reasons of his own, the cat had shown an interest in Balzac (in English), Emily Dickinson, and Zane Grey. Now he was on a Shakespeare kick. A complete set of the annotated plays in individual volumes had been given to Qwilleran by Polly, and they were a convenient format for pushing off a shelf. *Othello* and *Hamlet* had been Koko's selections in the last week.

After a dramatic reading of Hamlet's scene with his father's ghost, Qwilleran said, "To be continued." Then he added, "Mrs. Fulgrove is coming!" She was the industrious, competent, trustworthy housekeeper who came to the barn to "fluff it up," as she said, between visits from the high-powered janitorial service. Qwilleran always tried to be absent when she was working; when he returned, he could expect a slight aroma of beeswax and whiffs of homemade metal polish — a simple compound of vinegar and salt — that reminded him of salad dressing.

It would be improved, he thought, with a touch of garlic, but he never mentioned the whimsical suggestion to the intensely serious housekeeper.

On this occasion he left Mrs. Fulgrove a note about a strange odor on the first balcony, instructed the Siamese to stay out of her way, and departed for the newspaper office.

Space was always reserved on page two for the "Qwill Pen" column, and Qwilleran always filed his copy as late as possible — mainly to incur the friendly wrath of his pal Junior Goodwinter, managing editor. After some mutual jibes, Junior showed him the page proofs of the bookstore coverage.

Shooting from a high stepladder, the photographer had caught a close-up of the bronze Winston in the lower left-hand corner and the new building in the background. For contrast there was a file-photo print of the 1850 bookstore that had burned down. Then there was a close-up of the vestibule doormat with its stern directive:

DON'T LET THE CAT OUT

In the background was the inner door, with Dundee peering through the glass. In another photo the bibliocat was sniffing a five-thousand-dollar copy of Hemingway's *Death in the Afternoon*.

Then Junior scanned the "Qwill Pen" copy and rang for the copyboy.

"Hi, Mr. Q! I've got your book here!" Kenneth said.

"The conference room's empty. Meet me there."

A few minutes later Qwilleran was autographing the book and scribbling an appropriate inscription while saying the usual "Hope you enjoy it."

"I've already read it twice! I learned a lot!" Kenneth said. "If there's anything I can help you with, Mr. Q, I have weekends off, and I'd do it for nothing, just for the experience. You know — legwork or anything like that."

"It's unprofessional to work for nothing, so get that idea out of your head," Qwilleran said. "So far, I've never needed a legman, but if I do . . . Give me your home phone."

Qwilleran had to devise a plan to stay out of Mrs. Fulgrove's way that afternoon. Lunch at the Luncheonette was the first solution. He said to Lois, "I hear you made a big hit with those camera cowboys from Down Below."

"Nice bunch o' boys. We had a lotta laughs. They took my picture."

"Right now your visage is being flashed on TV screens from coast to coast."

"Don't know about my visage. I thought they were shooting in my face."

From there Qwilleran went to the public library to kill an hour, researching Lord Byron (Violet's favorite poet) and Tasso, the Italian poet after whom she named her watchdog. Brimming with more information than he really wanted, he returned to the barn to see if Mrs. Fulgrove had solved the mystery. He found her note written with meticulous handwriting and correct spelling, but she had a grammatical habit that mystified him. She talked the same way. He called it "whichery."

Dear Mister: I found a banana peel in one of your shoes, which you should keep your closet door closed. I put your shoes in the shed to air out, which you should leave them till morning. — Mrs. Fulgrove

Before his dinner date with Violet, Qwilleran considered his wardrobe thoughtfully. Once upon a time he had lacked interest in sartorial style; appearing in public with Polly had changed all that. Now he had blazers in several colors, fashionwise shirts and ties, and more than one suit. Before dining out he and Polly would compare notes: "What are you wearing?" As a result, their ensembles never clashed, and friends said, "You two always look so good together!"

To play it safe on Friday night he wore his camel hair blazer with brown trousers, light tan shirt, and monochromatic striped necktie. It was a fortunate choice, since Violet appeared in a tailored suit of brilliant violet twill. No hat. Polly always wore a hat when dining in restaurants.

It had been Violet's idea — since she was helping Lisa at the ESP all afternoon — that she could drive downtown with Alden, Qwilleran would pick her up at the bookstore, and then he would drive her home to Hibbard House after dinner — for a glimpse of the famous building and a brief meeting with some of the residents. They all read the "Qwill Pen" column and were eager to meet Mr. Q.

When he arrived at the bookstore at five-thirty, everyone was working late in a desperate attempt to be ready for the public opening.

Members of the staff said, "You two look wonderful!"

Polly said in a polite voice, "Have a nice . . . dinner."

On the drive to the restaurant, Qwilleran asked if Violet had dined at the Grist Mill since returning to Moose County. She had not. He regaled her with the background of the owner, Liz Hart, and the maître d', Derek Cuttlebrink, who had played Lady Bracknell in the recent play.

"You make everything sound so interesting!" she declared. "I know you're going to write a fascinating book on Hibbard House!"

Derek greeted them with professional

éclat but managed to throw a questioning glance at Qwilleran and a speculative glance at the sixtyish woman.

When the menus were presented, Qwilleran asked his guest, "What are they having for dinner at Hibbard House tonight?"

"If anyone has gone fishing, Cook prepares their catch for dinner, but there's always a backup of shrimp or lobster in the freezer."

Skillfully, Qwilleran steered the table talk past domestic matters, personal chitchat, and the ordering of food. He said, "Violet, I've been looking forward to hearing the history of your colorful family. Don't be reticent! You promised to tell all. And I happen to have a tape recorder in my pocket." The following account was later transcribed:

My great-grandfather, Cyrus, came to this area when it was wilderness and when he was a young man filled with ambition. He had nothing but a sawyer's skills, but he had a genius for business. He eventually owned all the sawmills in towns along the coast — at the mouth of rivers and creeks, where logs were floated down from the forests.

Like certain other self-made men in the past, he was eccentric. He never learned to read and write. And he undertook to build a house unlike any other in the area — or anywhere! While other successful entrepreneurs were building mansions of brick or stone, Cyrus built his entirely of wood — bigger, more original, totally unsafe. In an era of candles and fireplaces, it would certainly burn down! But it has outlasted three generations of Hibbards.

My grandfather, Geoffrey, was educated in private schools and lived the life of a country gentleman. My father, Jesmore, went to Harvard and lived the life of a gentleman scholar. But they all lived in the frame house that was expected to burn down! I grew up there — and returned there after a career in teaching.

Violet motioned to have the recording device turned off and then said, "May I ask you a rude question, Qwill?"

"If you don't object to getting a rude answer."

"Have you ever been married?"

"Once. Briefly. The details are withheld

122

until the posthumous publication of my memoirs. How about you?"

"Almost . . . Early in my career I taught at an American university in Italy and almost married an Italian artist, but my father called me home because my mother was dying. I never went back. The rest of my teaching was done in this country."

Qwilleran asked, "What caused you to take early retirement?"

She paused before answering. "My father was dying, and exacted a promise that I would live in the Hibbard House and preserve what he considered a sacred trust. I'm the last remaining Hibbard."

Qwilleran said, "I'm beginning to understand why you want a book written on the Hibbard House. I'm willing to write it. I'll have John Bushland call you to make a date for photographs. And the K Fund will publish it."

After this solemn pledge there was a silence at the table, until Qwilleran asked, "Alden tells me you've named your watchdog Tasso. Is that because of your Italian adventure?"

"Do you know Tasso?" she asked eagerly.

"Only through Lord Byron's epic."

"I adore Byron! He's so romantic!"

"He's a little long-winded for me," Qwilleran confessed. "I have a short attention span. A sonnet is about my speed — fourteen lines."

"Have you written any sonnets, Qwill?"

"No, but I consider myself a connoisseur of the form. I maintain that a good sonnet should not only paint a picture, express an emotion, or declare a philosophy; the words should feel good in the mouth when read aloud. Consonants and vowels should fit together in a smooth way. I won't mention any names, but consider this line: *Earth has not anything to show more fair.* Then compare it with the sibilance of: *When to the sessions of sweet silent thought,* which is difficult to say without spitting. In fact, when I read it to my cat, he hissed — the way he does at a garden snake. . . . But I digress. We were talking about the Hibbard House. Do you happen to have any pictures of the exterior? I've never seen it."

"I have a snapshot in my handbag."

After some fumbling, Violet extracted a print that had Qwilleran struggling to compose himself. He had heard it called historic, unique, impressive, original, or just HUGE! No one had called it handsome or even attractive. Now he knew why. The celebrated Hibbard House was *ugly*.

Diplomatically, he said, "I'm not completely familiar with architectural styles. Do you know what Hibbard House represents?"

"My grandfather, Geoffrey, called it eclectic."

"Did he tell you who designed it?"

"He said that no one designed it, it just happened. Cyrus bought thirty acres in the Middle Hummocks and took a crew of carpenters to see the property. There was an elevation in the center of the site, and that's where he wanted them to build him a large, square, three-story house with a pyramid-shaped roof and an observation tower rising from the peak. He wanted several large brick chimneys, several verandas both upstairs and downstairs, a grand front entrance with four columns, and a ballroom on the third floor."

"I see," Qwilleran said, stroking his moustache. "Shall we order dessert? I recommend the plum buckle."

The nighttime approach to the Hibbard House was along an unlighted country road in the wooded hummocks, and it loomed suddenly on its little hill, floodlighted and weird, in Qwilleran's opinion.

"Will you come in and meet some of the

guests, if they're still around?" Violet suggested.

She had left instructions for all the lights to be turned on, and she suggested a walk through the main rooms to get the effect.

It was unreal — a movie set, a fairy tale. "Enchanting!" he said.

He was sure it was staged, probably by Alden Wade, who was playing the piano in the music room. Someone was reading in the library. A bridge game was in progress in the drawing room, and one of the players waved to Qwilleran; she was the cats' veterinarian. Two young men were coming upstairs from the Ping-Pong table on the lower level; Violet introduced them as "our duck hunters"! They invited him to go hunting with them some Sunday.

"I'm a washout with a rifle," he said, "but I'd be interested in duck habitat as a topic for the 'Qwill Pen.' "

"We've got a book at the office you can borrow. We'll dig it out."

And Alden went on playing Chopin. What a ham! was Qwilleran's reaction.

There was a tall, erect older man with snow-white hair who was introduced as Judd Amhurst, a retired engineer. "He keeps us out of trouble," Violet said, giving him an appreciative look.

"I know who he is!" said Amhurst. "I'm one of his avid fans. I won a yellow pencil in one of his contests!"

The two men shook hands. "Have another pencil!" Qwilleran reached into his inside coat pocket for one of the fat wooden gold-stamped "Qwill Pen" pencils that he always carried.

"Wait'll the boys at the bar hear this!" Judd said.

"He never drinks anything stronger than Squunk water," Violet said, giving Judd a playful nudge.

"Are you hooked, too?" Qwilleran asked.

They pumped hands again, this time exchanging the fraternal handshake known only to "Squunkers."

Qwilleran found the retired engineer congenial. So did Violet, apparently.

She said he had known her father and might be able to supply material for the book.

Qwilleran told Violet they should get together for dinner again and discuss Wordsworth and Chekhov.

After his dinner with the heiress of the Hibbard estate, Qwilleran wrote the following in his personal journal:

127

Friday, September 26 — Why did I agree to write a book on that residential monstrosity? It's not only grotesque on the outside but hard to photograph on the inside! I must be slipping! After seeing the dark woodwork and ponderous furnishings, I made a feeble effort to postpone the project, but the dear lady seemed in a hurry to proceed. Did she think that — after all these years — the place would burn down in the next week?

Her great fear, I learned, was that the property would fall into the hands of developers, who would tear it down and build condos and a shopping mall. The publication of a book would give it the status of a national treasure, and the county might legislate against the commercial exploitation of the site . . . but *national treasure*?

Anyway, I promised to line up the photographer ASAP and read the trunkful of documents she gave me. They go back to circa 1925. Maybe I'll have an assignment for Kenneth sooner than either of us expected.

 Later that night, Moira MacDiarmid called.

"Oh, Qwill! We saw Dundee on TV tonight. We're so proud of him!"

"He's an asset to the bookstore," Qwilleran said. "I don't know whether he'll increase the sale of books, but he'll surely promote the demand for marmalade cats! What can I do for you?"

"Our daughter, Kathie, has just flown in from Down Below to be maid of honor at her best friend's wedding tomorrow. She's dying to see Dundee in his new environment. She's the one who trained him for a public career, you know. But she has to fly back to school Sunday night, and we wondered if you could use your pull to sneak us in the back door of the bookstore Sunday afternoon."

"I have a key. No problem. What time?" he asked.

ELEVEN

Qwilleran had set his alarm early for Saturday morning expecting Opening Day at the bookstore to be more of a problem than a success. He first phoned Polly in Indian Village, but a message on her answering machine said that she could be reached at the bookstore anytime after eight a.m.

Store hours started at nine-thirty, leading Qwilleran to deduce that she had left home very, very early . . . or had spent the night in downtown Pickax — at the hotel or at a friend's apartment or (not likely) in a sleeping bag on the floor of her office.

He phoned The Pirate's Chest and listened to a message: "Store hours are nine-thirty to five."

He started the coffeemaker and fed the cats, but they showed no interest in the preparation of their food. Nervously they hopped on and off the kitchen counter, staring through the window with ears pricked to an angle denoting Full Alarm!

Stepping outdoors, Qwilleran realized the source of their anxiety. To the west, toward Main Street, there was a constant hum of traffic punctuated by the screaming and blasting of police and emergency vehicles. He grabbed his orange hat, press card, and cell phone and headed for the action.

The road through the woods debouched into the theatre parking lot. It was jammed! Main Street was clogged with cars, and all curbs were parked bumper to bumper, legally or illegally. Sidewalks were thronged with pedestrians who had left their cars in the parking lots of churches and library and county buildings and were streaming toward the center of town.

Qwilleran pushed through the crowd, barking, "Coming through! Step aside, please!"

People made way for him joyfully. They were in a holiday mood. They said, "Hi, Mr. Q! Takin' Koko to meet Dundee?" They were on their way to see a real pirate's chest, a sculpture of Winston, a live bibliocat, and a five-thousand-dollar book.

Qwilleran continued on his way through the crowd, stopping once to shelter in a doorway and call on his cell phone.

"You're in early," he said when Polly answered.

"Everyone's here to plan our strategy," she said with her usual calm. "All the staff is here, plus three security guards. The public will be admitted a few at a time and routed through the store, down the stairs to the ESP, and up the basement stairs to the north parking lot."

"Where will Dundee be?"

"In the show window to the south of the entrance, along with displays of books, his cushion, his rag doll, and his toothbrush. People lining up to be admitted will pass the window and swoon over the charming scene. Indoors, the guards will say, 'Keep moving, folks! Ten thousand more are waiting to get in!' " She said it without excitement, as if it had been in the textbook on how to run a bookstore.

"Would you let me know if there's anything I can do for you?"

"Thank you, Qwill, but Alden Wade is here to manage activity on the selling floor, Lisa has a crew of volunteers downstairs, and a young man from the Winston Apartments offered to run errands. He's rather scruffy but nice. He's a friend of Dundee's Peggy. It was her idea to put Dundee in the show window, out of harm's way."

"How does he feel about it?" Qwilleran asked, being accustomed to a male cat with pronounced ideas of his own.

"Dundee is very agreeable, very well adjusted."

"I see. . . . Well, I'll phone you later if it won't be an intrusion."

"Not at all!" Polly sounded so businesslike.

Qwilleran turned around and went home. She had all the help she needed.

At the barn the Siamese digested their breakfast as they lay in a patch of sunlight — a triangle of sunlight that was created by one of the odd-shaped windows. In a few minutes it would move away, to their mystification, and they would crawl to a new sunny venue without really waking up.

Qwilleran made a fresh cup of coffee and tackled Violet's trunkful of documents representing a century of life in the ancestral mansion. Her scholarly father had reduced the collection from thousands to hundreds and placed them in chronological order. Even so, it would require a prodigious amount of research. Qwilleran phoned Kenneth and left a message.

The young man called back in a few minutes, somewhat out of breath. "Hi, Mr. Q! I've been doing errands for Mrs. Duncan — coffee and stuff, you know. What's up?

Something interesting, I hope."

"I think you'll find it so. It's a research project. It would mean scouting a trunkful of old papers, looking for material to be used in a book."

"I like it already! When do I start?"

"Yesterday. We have a short deadline. As soon as the traffic problem eases up, I'll deliver the trunk. I also recommend a dinner conference, if you're free. Onoosh's Café has booths and a little privacy. Do you like Mediterranean fare?"

"I've never had any. Lockmaster had a Mediterranean place called Ports of Call, but we always hung out at the Green Turnip."

"I hesitate to inquire about their menu," Qwilleran said.

"It's just a burger joint, but it was named after a horse. Green Turnip never won any races, but everybody loved him."

The deal was made. The time was set.

Kenneth said, "If it's the kind of restaurant where I should have a haircut, the girl next door will give me one."

Qwilleran said, "It might be a good idea."

 At five o'clock, when the bookstore doors were supposed to be closed,

Qwilleran phoned Polly and was not surprised to hear a weary voice.

"Qwill, I'm exhausted! The lineup of sightseers has been constant for almost eight hours — not that I do floor duty, but the mere presence of all those people wears one down. Do you understand? I was hoping we could have dinner tonight, but I'm afraid . . ."

"That's perfectly all right, Polly."

Considering his dinner conference, it was not only all right but highly advisable! He had known her long enough to predict her reactions. She disapproved of the trivial books that he wrote, calling them a waste of his true talent. And she would consider a book on the questionable Hibbard House to be the ultimate in trivia. She could never understand that Qwilleran considered himself a reporter, not a critic. It was a reporter's job to report, he maintained. In his early days he had been a crime reporter; now he reported on life as it was lived 400 miles north of everywhere. The Hibbard House was no architectural gem, but it was part of Moose County history, to be treated objectively and with more understanding than ridicule.

In Violet's trunk there was an envelope of family photos, and Qwilleran selected four — to represent the four-generation dynasty of individualists.

Cyrus as an old man, with a cane in each hand and a shawl over his head.

Geoffrey, the country gentleman, in riding attire, with a whip looped in his hand.

Jesmore, the gentleman scholar, in tweeds, seated in an impressive library.

Violet, the professor, in cap and gown, holding a large volume — probably Byron's poems.

"Yow!" came a shattering announcement in Qwilleran's ear. Time for dinner.

At Onoosh's, Kenneth was impressed by the brass-topped tables, beaded chandeliers, and exotic aromas — and also the attention accorded his host. Onoosh came out of the kitchen in her chef's toque to greet them, and the waitstaff seemed overjoyed.

Qwilleran asked his guest, "What will you have to drink while we're ordering dinner?"

"What are you having?"

"A Q cocktail, nonalcoholic. It's Squunk water with a dash of cranberry juice."

"Doesn't sound good, but I'll try it."

"Live dangerously," Qwilleran said.

"Meanwhile, I suppose you wonder what this is all about. Do you have a notebook or tape recorder?" First he explained the project: a book to be published by the K Fund about the historic Hibbard House built in the 1850s — the oldest frame structure in the county, occupied by four generations of Hibbards.

"Your job," he said to Kenneth, "will exercise your news sense, looking for 'the story' instead of statistics. The stories will be buried in that trunk I delivered to you: letters, documents, and news clips. What happened to the Hibbard family in a century and a half? How were they affected by wars, great storms, epidemics, accidents, crimes? But also look for honors awarded and prizes won, weddings and funerals, parties and hobbies. Get the idea?"

"Got it!" Kenneth said. "I can hardly wait to get started."

"Now let's look at the menu."

He suggested hummus as an appetizer . . . then lamb shish kebab and spanakopita, with baklava for dessert.

Then over cups of Greek coffee Qwilleran determined to satisfy his curiosity about "Whiskers," as Kenneth was called — without prying. The young man seemed reluctant to talk about himself, but little by little the following facts evolved:

He liked the Winston Park apartments. Everyone was young. The rent was reasonable. He could walk to work. He didn't have a car. The Luncheonette was just around the corner. He liked the people at the bookstore. Everyone was friendly, even the cat.

"Do you like cats?" Qwilleran asked.

"I don't know. We just had barn cats on the farm. We had mostly dogs and horses. Where did Dundee get his name?"

"In a nutshell: Orange cats are called marmalades, and Dundee is a Scottish city, long famous for orange marmalade. Do you know why it's an old tradition for bookstores to have cats? Think about it."

Kenneth said, "I suppose . . . for the same reason we had barn cats — to get rid of rodents."

"Right! Do you still visit your farm?"

After some hesitation Kenneth said, "The farm was sold. Both my parents are dead."

"Sorry to hear that," Qwilleran murmured. He could think of other questions, but Kenneth showed signs of withdrawal. So Qwilleran asked, "Anything more you need to know regarding your assignment?"

"About newsworthy items — what do I

do with them when I find them?"

"Give each one a reference number. Put it in a separate box. List the item and its reference number on a chart."

"I'll start tomorrow!"

TWELVE

Sunday, noon. The Siamese had enjoyed their midday snack and were washing up when Qwilleran sat down at the desk to find a number in the phone directory. Immediately, Yum Yum sprang to the desktop and assumed a hostile pose. How did she know he was about to call Fran Brodie? The two females had been feuding since Day One.

Fran was the most glamorous woman in town, a talented member of the theatre club, the police chief's daughter, and second in command at Amanda's Studio of Interior Design.

She answered the phone in a sulky, morning-after voice.

With forced enthusiasm he said, "Fran, let me extend belated compliments on your performance as Gwendolen!"

"Thank you. Too bad they had to cancel the show. . . . I hear you're starting an amazing new project!"

"Where did you hear it?"

"Never mind where. Say it isn't so. That

140

ancient monstrosity!"

In a tone of authority he said, "Elsewhere they have George Washington's oak tree and Benjamin Franklin's printing press. We have the Hibbard House! Yours not to criticize. It rose from the sawdust of a million trees a century and a half ago, in spite of fire, flood, hurricane, and decorating snobs." He knew that it irritated her to hear interior design called "decorating."

"All right. What's on your mind, if anything," she said in a huff of her own.

"I understand the rooms are large, dark, and over-furnished. Do you have any advice for John Bushland, who will have to photograph them?"

"Amanda helped them with their furnishings when Jesmore was alive. I've done a few things for Violet. I don't know where to start."

He said in a more agreeable voice, "Just give me a few tips for photographing, and I'll make notes for Bushy. Otherwise, I won't bother you except to ask you what you think of Alden Wade."

"That guy," she replied with unbridled admiration, "is not only a ball of fire but talented, handsome, and sexy!"

"I'm glad he has your approval, Fran."

Qwilleran wondered what had happened

to Dr. Prelligate, president of the community college and number one on Fran's list. What had happened to all the others? What would Chief Brodie have to say about his fickle daughter?

The MacDiarmids, mother and daughter, were expected at one o'clock, and Qwilleran walked to the bookstore in advance. Dundee was in the show window, sunning on his cushion, and nonchalantly accepting the plaudits of passersby.

When the MacDiarmids arrived and the door was unlocked, the feline celebrity came running.

"He knows me!" Kathie cried, blubbering tears of joy on his marmalade fur. She was tall like her father and had marmalade hair like her mother. She carried Dundee around as they looked at the real pirate's chest, the special doormat in the vestibule, and the show window where Dundee had charmed the mob the day before. Downstairs the ESP room was locked, but they could look through the glass panel and see the jelly cupboard with its fortune in rare books.

Moira said, "We must watch the time. Kathie has to catch a plane."

"Would you have time to walk around

the corner to Granny's Sweet Shop? She's famous for her banana splits," Qwilleran told them.

Granny was a real grandmother whose grandchildren all worked in the store and seemed to be a happy crew. Chairs and tables were the old soda-fountain style, with twisted wire legs and backrests.

Kathie ordered a banana split, and while her elders ate their sundaes, she kept looking across the room; then she whispered to her mother. Moira looked in the same direction and shook her head. Kathie persisted. "I know it's Wesley. He's grown a beard."

Qwilleran looked across the room casually and said, "His name is Kenneth. He's a copyboy at the *Something*." By the time the visitors left for the airport, Kenneth had gone.

Qwilleran asked Granny about Saturday's business.

"Never saw anything like it!" she cried, slapping her forehead. "They were lined up waiting to get in all day! We ran out of ice cream at three o'clock and had to close the doors."

Then he asked, "Do you get much business, ordinarily, from the Winston Park apartments?"

"Oh, yes! They're nice young people! Always over here drinking ice-cream sodas and malts. Better than a lot of other things they could drink."

"The two young people who went out a few moments ago looked familiar to me," Qwilleran said.

"Peggy's her name. They call him Whiskers. Nice kids."

Qwilleran had noticed that Peggy picked up the check; Kenneth turned away with his hands in his pockets while she was paying.

Qwilleran walked home, and when he reached the barnyard he could see a cat in the kitchen window, standing on his hind legs in a state of frenzy. The man was well acquainted with feline telepathy. One frantic cat in the window signified a voice on the answering machine. Two frantic cats meant "Feed us! We're famished!"

The phone call was from Alden Wade: "Qwill, let me know if you need anything special for your talk next Thursday. Lectern? Easel? Projector and screen? Dancing girls?"

Qwilleran groaned and muttered a thank-you. He had forgotten entirely about the first meeting of the literary club! He thought fast.

There was much he could say about the colorful old bookseller, but he needed visuals to rivet audience attention: large-size photos projected on the wall behind the platform.

He phoned Kenneth. "Do me a favor tomorrow when you get to the paper. Look in the photo file for glossies of the late Eddington Smith, his bookstore, and his cat. Winston was on the front page after the fire . . . also any pix there might be of the burning building."

"I can handle that! Want them delivered somewhere?"

"Just leave them in my name on Junior Goodwinter's desk. Tell him I'll pick them up when I file my Tuesday copy."

"I can handle that."

"I saw you at Granny's, Ken. Did you have one of her famous banana splits?"

"Yeah. Peggy was buying. I made some deliveries for her."

"Good-looking woman! Is she the one who's Dundee's valet?"

"Yeah. She loves it! She'd pay for the fun of doing it. . . . Did you like how she cut my hair, Mr. Q?"

"Couldn't have done better myself."

Qwilleran wondered who cut Peggy's hair. Her bangs came too low over her eyebrows.

Next he phoned Thornton Haggis, county historian replacing Homer Tibbitt, historian emeritus.

"Thorn, does the historical collection at the library have any decent old shots of Edd Smith and/or his property? Just give me an idea; I'll pick them up."

"I'm pretty sure, but I'll take a look. Is that for your lit club speech? My wife and I are going. She behaves like a groupie at your speeches. I tell her she only goes to see your Mark Twain moustache."

"Good! I won't work so hard on my script," Qwilleran said. "And I'll tell the barber not to trim my major attraction."

He said to the cats, "Your uncle Bushy is coming over this afternoon, but there's no need to go and hide; he's not bringing his camera."

The commercial photographer, John Bushland, lived on nearby Pleasant Street with his new wife, Janice, and their four Amazon parrots. They were getting together to discuss the Hibbard House.

It was a calm, pleasant afternoon, so they took a tray of refreshments out to the

146

octagonal gazebo, screened on all eight sides. The cats went along in their canvas tote bag.

Janice said, "It's luscious out here! . . . Bushy, could we have something like this next summer?"

Her husband, whose hair was steadily receding, liked his irreverent nickname.

Qwilleran asked, "How are the parrots adapting to a new ménage?"

"They're fascinated by my shiny head," the photographer said.

"And we have two kittens from the brood next door!" his wife said with excitement. "One brownish and one calico."

"Have you been able to point the camera at them?"

"Anytime we feel like it," Bushy said. "They're not fussy, as long as they get their two squares a day. . . . Now tell me about the slides you mentioned on the phone."

Qwilleran asked, "How long will it take to make slides from black-and-white photos?"

"I can get them whenever I want them. I can pull strings, and I have a projector you can use. In fact, I'll operate it for you. What's it for?"

Qwilleran explained the forthcoming program for the literary club, and Bushy thought he might have shots of Edd Smith in his file. He remembered one of the old man on the top step of a high stepladder, and another of him feeding pigeons on the sidewalk.

Then they tackled the question of photographing the Hibbard House.

Bushy said, "When I phoned Miss Hibbard to make an appointment for the shoot, she invited me to see the interior in advance. The rooms are huge, dark, and cluttered! Believe me, this is not going to be an easy assignment!"

Qwilleran told Janice, "I've never heard a photographer admit that anything would be easy. They're a smart breed. When the pictures turn out to be super, they're heroes."

She squealed with amusement, then said, "He took me along for the ride when he went to check the quality of light on the exterior. It's very strange architecture! What style is it supposed to be? I thought I'd seen everything when I lived in California."

"Well, according to Fran Brodie, it has a colonial entrance, a Gothic roof, and a Venetian tower. The Victorian verandas were added later. The interiors, Fran says, are basically Jacobean."

Bushy said, "I've told Violet — she told me to call her that — to have a lot of fresh white flowers in the place and put a white tablecloth on the big dining table. I also told her we won't be using people in the pix."

Janice said, "I'm going along as his assistant."

"Yeah, she's been training, and she's very good! There are two things to be learned on this job: the use of close-ups when long shots are impractical . . . and the use of indirect lighting. In my van I have large white reflecting boards, and we'll bounce the light off them."

Then the two men entertained Janice with tales of their early acquaintance when Bushy lived in Lockmaster.

"I'm glad I moved to Pickax," he said.

"All the best people come here from Lockmaster," Qwilleran told him. "The latest is Alden Wade. He's really taking the town by storm. . . . Do you know Alden, Bushy?"

"Only by reputation!" It was said in a snide manner that alerted Qwilleran's curiosity.

Janice said, "We saw him in the play, and he was wonderful! He's going to teach a class in acting, I've heard. I'd love to enroll!"

"Incidentally, he lives at Hibbard House," Qwilleran said.

"Yow-ow!" came an emphatic announcement from Koko, who had been watching crows through the screens.

Janice jumped up. "He wants his dinner, and it's time for us to go home and feed Bonnie and Clyde. Bushy named the kittens that because they're embarking on a life of crime."

She excused herself and ran indoors, and Qwilleran walked with the photographer to the barnyard. "I've been hearing scuttlebutt about Alden, Bushy. It concerns me because Polly has hired him to handle special events for the bookstore. He's the one who asked me to speak to the new literary club."

"Yeah . . . well . . . I guess he knows his stuff, but he's got a reputation as a home breaker."

"The good-looking guys are always suspect, aren't they?"

"I dunno. I was never a good-looking guy." He passed his hand over his bald head. "But Alden has a track record."

THIRTEEN

It was Monday morning, and The Pirate's Chest was officially open for business. Furthermore, Qwilleran had promised to buy the first book at Eddington Smith's Place. He had to be there with a fat checkbook, and it had to be fatter than he thought.

Meanwhile, the Siamese were fed early, and he himself grimly prepared a bowl of cereal and sliced bananas, monitored by Koko sitting atop the bar.

At nine-thirty Lisa was waiting with the key to the jelly cupboard for the first customer. "I knew you wouldn't want publicity, Qwill, but it would have made a front-page story — 'Prominent citizen buys rare book for his cat to open ESP!' but then you'd have to have Koko here, too, and he might not get along with Dundee."

"You're dreaming, Lisa!"

"Violet wanted to be here, but she has a doctor's appointment in Lockmaster.

151

Someone is driving her there."

"I hope she's not unwell."

"It's just an ongoing thing that she has to check occasionally. I think they'll have lunch at Inglehart's and make a party out of it. Are you ready?" She drew the precious book from the cupboard and handed it to her first customer.

It was the usual size of a child's book, with a glossy paper jacket in bright blue and a cartoon of a cat with a tall hat striped in white and red. The sixty-odd pages had storytelling verses and more cartoons.

"Will Koko like it?" Lisa asked.

"He likes thin books because they're easy to push off the shelf. So much for his literary taste! But this one will be locked up and displayed occasionally on the coffee table, where he'll sit on it as an expression of respect. He senses when a book is valuable."

Looking unconvinced, Lisa said, "Well . . . if you say so! . . . And now I have a surprise for you! Violet has asked me to break the news. . . . Her father was a great admirer of the journalism profession, and he collected books written by and about journalists — forty or fifty titles —"

"I'll buy them!" Qwilleran interrupted,

pulling out his checkbook.

"No! She's giving them to you as a thank-you for doing the book about the Hibbard House!"

"Tell her to give the whole caboodle to the ESP — and then I'll buy them. She'll get a tax break, I'll get the chance of a lifetime, and ESP will get a big contribution. It's simple arithmetic! Are the books here?"

"No. They're at the house — four or five boxes of them. She intended that Alden could deliver them to your barn later this afternoon."

"I'll be there. I'll write a check to ESP. You and Violet can decide how much."

Qwilleran walked home with *The Cat in the Hat*. Lisa had put it in one of the plastic bags donated by the drugstore. When he entered the barnyard, both cats were cavorting in the kitchen window, no doubt expecting some meat loaf from Lois's. At any rate, they were disappointed when the rare book was presented — sniffing, looking up in mystification, and sniffing again in apparent disbelief. Even Koko, the chief bibliocat, had no interest in the new acquisition.

That Koko! Qwilleran muttered to himself; he'd probably rather have *The Life of George Washington*!

He went back downtown to do errands, and there, in front of the Sprenkle Building, he saw Maggie Sprenkle looking up and down Main Street.

"Waiting for a streetcar?" he asked.

"Oh, Qwill!" She laughed. "You always cheer me up. I couldn't make up my mind where to go first — post office or bank."

"Considering the way the postage rates are going up," he advised, "go to the bank first. . . . You're looking fine, Maggie. How are your ladies?" He noted cat hairs on her dark blue outfit; she was a dedicated cat hugger.

"Our dear Charlotte died of old age, and we miss her, but we have a little gray lady from the humane shelter. We call her Emily. Would you like to come up and meet her and have a cup of tea?"

"I'd like to go up and discuss something with you . . . but no tea, thanks. I've just had three cups of coffee." It was a fib but a nice way of refusing Maggie's weak jasmine tea — with one or more cat hairs floating in it.

The Sprenkle Building dated from the early years when merchants sold their goods on the ground floor and raised large families on the upper floors. Now there were real estate and insurance offices on the ground floor, while Maggie lived in a Victorian palace on the second and third levels. After the death of her husband, Jeremy, she had sold their country house, parted with his lavish rose gardens, and moved downtown, close to her numerous volunteer efforts.

She asked Qwilleran if he wanted to walk up the front stairs or go around to the elevator in the rear. The stairs were steep and narrow in the old style, and thick carpet made the shallow treads even shallower for a size-twelve shoe. The elevator, accessible from the parking lot in the rear, had been a recent innovation.

"I'm feeling reckless — I'll take the dangerous shortcut," he said.

The stairs were carpeted with red roses; the walls were deep red, hung with myriad framed engravings. The interior designer, Amanda Goodwinter, had explained to Qwilleran, "I give the customers what they want! It's their money, and they have to live with it."

Upstairs there were more red roses wall to wall and more red walls hung with large oil paintings in gilt frames.

The discussion took place at a richly carved marble-top table around which were velvet-tufted chairs.

"Sure you don't want a cup of tea?" Maggie asked.

Qwilleran declined again and began: "I'm writing a book on the Hibbard House, to be published by the K Fund —"

"I know! Violet told me! I'm delighted! Is there any way I can help? I'm older than she is, but we grew up together."

"A perfect setup, Maggie! I'm collecting memories of Hibbard House from long-time residents of the community." He placed a pocket-size tape recorder on the marble table.

"Oh, I remember going up in the tower to see the lake ten miles away . . . and tobogganing down the Hibbard hill in winter . . . camping out in sleeping bags on an upstairs veranda in summertime . . . sitting around the fire in the library while Violet's father read to us.

"She went away to college and then to Italy, but I married my Jeremy and was deliriously happy. He loved growing roses, and every day he would bring me one perfect floribunda from the garden and sing 'Only a Rose' from the Rudolf Friml operetta! He had a beautiful baritone voice! . . .

Violet and I corresponded while she was in Italy, and I was thrilled to hear she was marrying an artist over there. But when her parents found out that he wasn't only an artist but a *foreigner* . . . they had fits! Violet was told it would kill her mother! She came home."

"And never married?" Qwilleran asked.

Maggie nodded soberly. "Out of spite, I think. She was an only child, and it meant the end of the direct Hibbard bloodline. . . . But I'll never forget how she cried, day after day, when she first came home from Italy. I cried with her!"

Tears welled in Maggie's eyes, and Qwilleran said, "I believe I would like a cup of tea."

When Maggie returned with the tea tray, her face was composed.

"I felt doubly sorry for Violet because Jeremy and I were blissfully married and he was raising roses with a passion. Then one day he sent her a single long-stemmed rose with the famous Hāfez of Shīrāz poem that you probably know." She recited the lines from the thirteenth-century poem:

Give never the wine bowl from thy hand
Nor loose thy grasp on the rose's stem
'Tis a mad bad world that the fates have planned.

"*Mmm,*" Qwilleran murmured. "An inspired gesture!"

"It was just what she needed, Qwill. I don't know whether it was the poem or the rose. Jeremy started rose-watching twenty years before it became fashionable in Lockmaster. He raised long-stemmed roses for the purpose, in a hothouse. They're a special hybrid, you know, planted close together so they grow tall. I wish you and Jeremy could have known each other.

"Do you know about Violet's health problem, Qwill?"

"I know she went to Lockmaster for a checkup today."

"She's known for several years that she has an aneurysm. It could strike her down without warning."

For a moment Qwilleran could only stare. "I'm shocked! And greatly saddened! And amazed that she faces the world with such poise and enthusiasm."

"She's learned to make the most of every day," Maggie said. "And so you know why I'm glad that you're working on a Hibbard House book. On the other hand, she could live to be one hundred. I'll think of some more early memories."

"Keep adding them to the tape, Maggie, and I'll check back with you in a week."

🐾 When Alden, in the official Hibbard House van, pulled into the barnyard, Qwilleran went out to suggest backing up to the kitchen door for efficient unloading. Koko and Yum Yum were watching in the kitchen window but scattered. Qwilleran liked to say that only two Siamese know how to scatter in three directions at once.

The men carried the boxes to one side of the fireplace cube, where Alden offered to help shelve the books.

Qwilleran said, "Since they're going to be catalogued first, I'll unpack, and you go up the ramp to check out the acoustics of this dump. Recite some Shakespeare."

"Chance of a lifetime!" his guest declared as he faced a complete set of Shakespeare plays in individual volumes. "I see you have the Arden collection, you lucky dog!"

"Take *Henry the Fifth* and read the prologue," Qwilleran suggested. Then he listened with genuine fascination as thirty-four lines resounded from the roof of the barn, starting with "O! for a Muse of fire . . ."

The barn had never sounded so good! Perhaps the actor had never sounded so good!

"Sing something, Alden!" he shouted from the ground floor.

Alden sang, "Give me some men who are stout-hearted men . . ."

Qwilleran applauded, and with exaltation Alden started back down the ramp. Within seconds his feet shot up, and he landed with an ominous thump.

Shouting, Qwilleran raced up the slope, seeing a blur of fur disappear as he did so. "Alden! Are you hurt? What happened?"

"I don't know, but I'm all right. In theatre studies we teach how to fall onstage."

"How about a little drink for your nerves?"

"My nerves are okay. Thanks, but I have to get home to uncork the wine."

"Tell Violet I'm writing a profuse thank-you note!"

Qwilleran was glad the drink had been declined; he wanted to start organizing his bonanza of journalists, bridging the late nineteenth and early twentieth centuries. There were names like Mencken, Hearst, Patterson, and Luce . . . women like

Nellie Bly and Ida Tarbell . . . Mark Twain, Artemus Ward, Irvin S. Cobb, Will Rogers, George Ade, Stephen Crane, Ambrose Bierce, and more.

The Siamese were encroaching on the scene, sniffing inquisitively. But Koko walked with that peculiar stiff-legged gait denoting guilt, leading Qwilleran up the ramp to the scene of the crash, and there — as he might have suspected — was a narrow strip of banana peel.

Thinking about it later, over a cup of coffee, Qwilleran had to chuckle when he thought of Alden's nasty spill. Since the beginning of burlesque there had been humor in slipping on a banana peel. Putting two and two together, he had to conclude that Koko simply did not like Alden Wade, despite his fine speaking voice and polished manners. In fact, Qwilleran was inspired to compose a parody of the well-known Samuel Johnson verse:

He does not like thee, Mr. Wade,
No explanation has been made.
I only know
The status quo.
He does not like thee, Mr. Wade.

FOURTEEN

Before Qwilleran could automate the coffeemaker on Tuesday morning, Bushy phoned. "Hey, Qwill! Just wanted you to know I spent the day shooting Hibbard exteriors yesterday. It was a good day for exteriors. Miss Hibbard wasn't around, but I didn't need her. Today I'm taking Janice, and we're doing interiors."

Qwilleran said, "You mean, you don't want me for a flunky this time? I'm fired?"

"You're fired! I'll have the services of a housekeeper and houseboy all day. But I'm taking Janice along as official note taker because she's dying to see the place.

"Now . . . about those photos for the lit club: Are you picking them up from the newspaper today?"

"Want me to drop them off at your house tonight?" Qwilleran asked.

"If you will. I'd pick 'em up but I have an assignment for the paper."

"You're working your head off, Bushy! If

you didn't work so hard, maybe you'd grow more hair."

"And I'm not even getting rich. . . . So I'll tell Jan to expect you."

Qwilleran himself was pressed for time. He had a "Qwill Pen" deadline at noon and had not given it a single thought. On such occasions there were a few tricks of the trade he could use: feature a "Readers Write" column, rounding up opinions, ideas, and complaints from the general public . . . or pull a page from his private journal and stretch it to a thousand words.

Another chore Qwilleran faced this week was a speech for the literary club.

He handed in his patchwork column before the deadline, picked up Kenneth's envelope of Edd Smith photos, and checked out the library's historical collection of ancient photographs. There were several pictures of the old bookseller and his old building and trusty old book-dusting cat. Winston had several predecessors, but they all looked like the same one: gray, shaggy, and feathery of tail.

Then Qwilleran went home to the barn to work on his address for the literary club. He never read a speech in front of an audience. Rather, he made notes to jog his memory — and ad-libbed.

Now he stretched out in a lounge chair with a pad and pencil. First he had to recollect everything he knew about Edd Smith; they had been friends ever since Qwilleran arrived in Pickax and became addicted to old books. Every time he walked downtown he would swing around behind the post office and visit the quaint store — browsing, buying a book or two, and taking a can of sardines to Winston. Edd came to consider him a "best friend," confiding in him about his family history. Could his tales be believed? He was descended from pioneers, who were storytellers and jokesters by nature. What they said could be true or invented or whimsical humor, factual or exaggerated.

Now Qwilleran had to decide how much to tell his Thursday audience. The notes he made on his pad included: Old oak tree . . . book scouts . . . Edd's handgun . . . liver and onions . . . "Call the police" . . . Edd's old truck . . . and perhaps his grandmother's scandalous secret, true or false.

As Qwilleran reminisced, he was aware that Koko was sitting nearby in a compact bundle, concentrating, as if helping him to remember. The man was not the first who credited a family cat with helping him find the right word, an elusive idea, or a forgotten detail.

As for the photos of Edd Smith that Bushy would make into slides, there was very little choice. They could be titled "Edd in front of shop with cat" and "Edd in front of shop without cat." It was always the same wooden pose and solemn expression; the bookseller merely grew older with the years, and so did his clothing.

His reveries were interrupted by a sudden "plop" as *Fables in Slang* fell off the shelf, while Koko crouched in the open space, looking downward. The book had fallen with covers splayed and pages open to a sketch titled "Sister Mae Who Did As Well As Could Be Expected."

This meant that Qwilleran had to read the story about Sister Mae aloud. Frankly, he was not enthusiastic about George Ade's slangy style or racy material, as they were described in 1899, and Koko dozed off before the reading was over.

It was a neat little book, the size of a modern paperback, but the binding was hardback covered in cloth that looked like fine tapestry. One wondered about the price of it in a period when the Sunday *New York Times* sold for five cents. All that aside, Qwilleran was sure Koko merely liked the book because it was so small. He put the volume back on the shelf and prepared the cats' evening meal.

After dinner, he took his manila envelope of Edd Smith photos to the house on Pleasant Street. Janice had inherited the mansion from her boss, the late Thelma Thackery, along with four Amazon parrots.

"Go into the aviary," Janice said, "and I'll bring a tray. I hope you didn't eat dessert. I've made apricot squares."

"I cannot tell a lie," Qwilleran said. "I had dessert, but I'm willing to overlook that fact and apply myself to apricot squares."

"Thelma always said you had nobility of character, Qwill."

The aviary occupied what had been the "second parlor" in earlier days. Chicken-wire fencing divided the room in two. On one side were the birds and their perches, toys, and private cages; the rest of the room was devoted to slouchy wicker furniture. "What's Bushy's assignment tonight?" Qwilleran asked.

"Scottish Night at the lodge hall."

"Did you have a good time today?"

"Fantastic! I've never seen such a house!"

"No one has!"

"All that carving — everywhere! The grand staircase — the fireplaces — the furniture — the picture frames! The dining table seats ten and was covered with a white cloth and set with fabulous china, crystal, and silver. In the middle were two bowls of flowers and three tall silver candlesticks. There were flowers everywhere, the way Bushy had requested. No matter how old a house, he says, cut flowers make it look new and fresh."

"Did you meet Miss Hibbard?" Qwilleran asked.

"Not until the afternoon. She was working at the ESP in the morning. I told her I had all the notes I needed and suggested we could just sit and talk for a while. Well! You wouldn't believe it, Qwill! We talked like a couple of young girls! And she's at least sixty! But we were both giggling and exchanging secrets. She wanted to know all about Bushy; said balding men are sexy. I told her we were newlyweds — and had a cabin cruiser and would like to take her for an outing some weekend. I said she could bring a date. That's when she got all flustered and said she also was a new bride!"

Qwilleran, for all his usual poise, almost choked on his coffee.

"I reacted the same way, Qwill, and struggled to stay cool. I didn't want to pry, and I asked questions all around the subject. She was dying to tell me but said it wouldn't be announced until Friday's paper — on the wedding page."

A whimsical thought drifted through Qwilleran's head: It would be ironic if Violet's new husband proved to be her long-ago Italian artist, back in her life. More likely, it was Judd Amhurst, amiable, handsomely white-haired, and a retired engineer. As operator of a large guest house, Violet would do well to have an engineer in the family. Unfortunately, Qwilleran realized he would have no intimate dinners now to discuss Wordsworth and Chekhov at the Grist Mill.

"I know you won't jump the gun, will you, Qwill? Violet wanted to change her will before the news leaks. She spent this morning at the lawyer's office — not the ESP."

He said, "There's nothing like a little duplicity to add spice to life. . . . Is that Bushy's car pulling in?"

They went to the back door to meet him, and the photographer unslung his gear.

"Are you full of Scotch and haggis?" Qwilleran asked.

"Nah, I don't touch that stuff. Got any coffee?"

They sat at the kitchen table with the photos of Edd, eliminating near-duplicates. It was more important, they decided, to have a dozen good shots and flash them on and off as background atmosphere.

Bushy said, "I went to the bookstore and looked at the meeting room. The wall behind the speaker is large and blank. I figure we shouldn't project slides sharply on a small screen but softly on the back wall, fading one in, holding it awhile, then fading it out. If we repeat a couple — okay. The visuals are for atmosphere only."

"Can I help at the meeting?" Janice interrupted. "I could follow your script, Qwill, and hand Bushy the suitable slide."

"I don't use a script," Qwilleran said. "But I'll give you a list of topics in sequence."

Then Qwilleran went home, threatening to take Bonnie and Clyde, who had been sitting on his lap, sniffing his ear, and otherwise making their presence felt.

As he entered the barn, it was nearing eleven p.m., the hour when Qwilleran used to call Polly or Polly used to call him. The pressures of her new job had dampened their camaraderie. He still shopped for her groceries once or twice a week, but she was always too busy or too tired for dinner dates, evenings of good music, or festive weekends.

Their get-togethers in recent weeks had been about inventory selecting and ordering and delivery of books. He had lived through all of Polly's anxieties about hiring and salaries. As Polly's best friend, he was expected to advise her about aisle widths and customer comfort. . . . As for classical music on the magnificent stereo system at the barn, she had been in no mood for relaxing moments. And now that the store was open and running, she was too excited to relax. What next?

The phone rang. It was exactly eleven o'clock and he always had the expectancy that it was Polly calling to get their nightly custom back on track.

But it was the police chief. "Got some news for you!" he said.

"Good or bad?"

"Weird."

"Why don't you pop over here for a wee dram," Qwilleran invited.

At the snack bar, where Andy liked to do his imbibing, he laid out a bottle of Scotch, ice cubes, a cheese tray, and a glass of Squunk water for himself. Then on the bar top just above, he put the rare cat book from the locked drawer, hoping Koko would demonstrate his taste in literature.

In a matter of minutes the big, burly Scot in khakis burst through the kitchen door. "Where's that smart cat? Got an assignment for him!"

"Sit down and pour yourself a nip, Andy. Did you play the pipe at Scottish Night?"

"Aye! You missed some good haggis!"

"So what's the news?"

"Theft at the ESP. A five-thousand-dollar book. A crook from Down Below, that's for sure — because of all that publicity on TV. We turned the case over to the state police."

"What was the title? Who was the author?"

"*Death in the Afternoon* by what's-his-name."

"Who reported it?"

"That new fella — Alden Wade. He works for Mrs. Duncan and volunteers for the Edd Smith outfit downstairs."

At that moment Koko, as if on cue, rose from the floor to the top of the bar with effortless grace and sat down on *his book*.

Qwilleran said, "That's his own book. I bought it for him on the first day they were open for business." No mention was made of the price; Brodie would have choked on his cheese.

"Good stuff. Tastes like Stilton."

"That's what it is!"

FIFTEEN

On Wednesday morning Qwilleran first fed the cats, a performance he repeated about seven hundred times a year. To make the ritual entertaining for himself, he spoke intelligently to them — a device said to raise their consciousness. Koko always listened thoughtfully with a slight inclination of his fine brown head; Yum Yum licked a certain spot on her chest.

On this occasion, Qwilleran tried a little Latin: *Sic transit gloria mundi . . . E pluribus unum . . . Tempus fugit.* It was not well received. Both cats toppled over on the floor and had a playful wrestling match. So much for higher education, Qwilleran decided.

He received a phone call while he was eating his own breakfast. Kenneth was calling from the newspaper.

"Hey, Mr. Q! Breaking news!" he said in a muffled voice. "Five-thousand-dollar book stolen! Same one Dundee was sniffing in the photo! It's gonna be on the front page!"

"That'll sell a few papers," Qwilleran

said. "Lucky it was the book they stole and not the cat."

"Yeah, well . . . I thought you'd want to know. . . . And I've finished your research, Mr. Q."

"Good! I'll pick up the trunk this evening."

"Peggy could drive me over with it. She's crazy to meet your cats!"

"What time?"

"Right after work."

"See you then." He had to chuckle over the hot breaking news. To Koko, who was hanging around waiting for a banana peel, he said, "Your cousin Kenneth is coming over and bringing Dundee's handmaiden, who wants to meet you." He wondered how Koko would react to the heavy bangs hanging almost to Peggy's eyebrows. To a cat they might look menacing, like a certain breed of dog.

He gave the Siamese a good brushing and then read to them from *Fables in Slang*, which came tumbling off the shelf again. The humor seemed no more captivating than before, and he looked up George Ade in the encyclopedia: "Popular humorist and playwright (1866–1944)."

Next he phoned the county historian. Thornton Haggis had his finger on the pulse of all the old-timers.

"What do you know about George Ade?" he asked Thorn.

"My sons drink it on the soccer field. It renews their energy. Why do you ask?"

"Bad joke, Thorn. . . . Are you and your wife attending the lit club meeting?"

"Wouldn't miss it. As I said before, she acts like a middle-aged groupie at your lectures. I think it's your moustache she goes for."

"I have another question. Did Haggis Monument Works do any gravestones for the Hibbard family?"

"We did 'em all! My grandfather, my father, and myself. They liked their headstones large, elaborate, and expensive. Why do you ask?"

"I'm writing a book about the Hibbard House, Thorn, and thought you might have some input."

"You can write a whole chapter on the subject. There's a private cemetery on their property, and I can show you a record book with names, dates, and sketches of the proposed monuments. We carved angels, baskets of flowers, baby lambs, portraits of the deceased, and some lengthy inscriptions, based on so much per letter. There was only one plain marker: a flat slab for a daughter who died in disgrace."

Qwilleran said, "This is great information, Thorn. I'll follow through. When the time comes, I'd like to see those account books. . . . Meanwhile, I saw something in the historic collection that only you would appreciate. The front page of an 1899 *New York Times*! It had been donated by Violet Hibbard's father. The headlines reported a bank robbery, a murder, a poisoning mystery, a fire in a manhole, and a billion-dollar corporate failure."

"Which proves," Thornton said, "that things don't get worse, they're only different."

Qwilleran said, "And just to show you how different, Thorn, the Sunday *Times*, twenty-two pages, sold for a nickel!"

Later in the day Qwilleran was in Toodle's Market, picking up fruit and vegetables for Polly and bananas for himself, when a voice said, "Mr. Q in person, I believe." He turned and saw a clean-cut man of about forty, who introduced himself as Bill Turmeric. He was the Sawdust City teacher of English who wrote entertaining letters to the "Qwill Pen" and the editorial page.

Qwilleran shook the proffered hand. "Glad to meet you! Have a banana. Dr.

Diane says they're good for you."

"My wife is always promoting them, too. Her aunt, by the way, won a dinner date with you in a charity auction a few years ago and has never stopped talking about it."

"Sarah Plensdorf," Qwilleran said. "Charming lady!"

"How are Koko and Yum Yum? I'm sure my kids would like to know."

"Koko is cool, and Yum Yum is sassy; sometimes the other way around." A small crowd of shoppers had gathered, listening and smiling, and he added, "Let's move out of the way so these good people can buy some bananas."

Once the two men and their shopping carts were in an open space, Qwilleran asked, "Do you have time for coffee? I'm treating."

"Best offer I've had all week."

At the coffee bar they sat on uncomfortable stools designed to discourage loitering, and Qwilleran said, "May I seize the moment and ask a question? . . . Is there such a thing as a 'dangling which'? My housekeeper says, 'My daughter is coming to visit, which I can't clean next Wednesday.' Is that Moose County patois?"

"No, it's a syntactical curiosity found elsewhere. The relative pronoun 'which' is used to introduce a clause that has no antecedent in the previous clause. It's used as a shortcut for 'and in connection with that, you might say . . .' Does that answer your question?"

"In connection with that, you might say . . . more or less" was Qwilleran's honest reply.

Wetherby Goode was among the callers that afternoon at the barn. He said, "When are you going to move back to the Village so I can give you the hot news over the back fence?"

"What's the hot news I don't already know?"

"Unit Two has been purchased — for sure, this time."

"By whom?"

"I'll drop in at the barn on my way to the station and tell you."

For the rest of the afternoon Qwilleran racked his brain without answers. Unanswered questions drove him into a quiet frenzy. And when the weatherman drove into the barnyard, he was met by his favorite drink on a silver tray. "Okay! Who is it?"

"Our veterinarian!"

"Dr. Constable? She lives at the Hibbard Guest House! Did you get this information from the same impeccable source that misled you last time?"

"I'm gullible. I even believe my own weather forecasts."

"What is her presumed reason for leaving the guest house?"

"She can't have pets there. Taking care of other people's animals and having none of her own is frustrating, she told the management at the Village. She'll have five resident patients in the Willows alone. I call that a neat situation, all the way around. We should give a big party for her when she arrives."

"Don't overreact, Joe. Not until we find out if she makes house calls in the middle of the night."

They went indoors and sat at the snack bar. Wetherby asked suddenly, "Are you someone's first husband?"

"Someone's first and last. Why do you ask?"

"My sister in Horseradish has recently divorced her first husband, and she's joined a First Husband's Club. The gals get together and bash their first husbands. She says they have a ball!"

"I can imagine," Qwilleran said. "I'd like to hear a recording of the proceedings."

"It's nothing nasty, only humorous."

"I see . . . Is this organization exclusive with Horseradish? Or does it have chapters countrywide?"

"So far, I believe it's purely local. You know they're mostly berserk in that town. . . . Well, I've got to get to the station. There's some violent weather in the offing."

As Qwilleran walked with Wetherby to his car, another vehicle pulled into the barnyard bringing Peggy, Kenneth, and the trunkful of research. The three persons were introduced.

"Oh, Mr. Goode!" she cried. "Your weathercasts are . . . so good!"

"Thanks. Call me Joe." He looked unusually pleased.

Peggy was wearing a slim-legged red jumpsuit and looked what Qwilleran considered "fetching." He said, "Peggy is chief assistant to Dundee, the bibliocat. I'm her understudy. Kenneth is the new copy facilitator at the newspaper."

"Wish I could stay," Wetherby said with genuine regret, "but I'm due at the station."

As he went to his car, he threw a backward glance at Peggy, and as Qwilleran escorted the young couple to the barn, she threw a backward glance at Wetherby.

"Shall I bring the trunk, Mr. Q?" Kenneth asked.

"Come in and see the barn first, and have some refreshments" was the answer.

"Oh, wow! Oh, wow!" said the copy facilitator, flinging his arms wide.

"If you want a thrill, go to the top of the ramp and see the view from there. But watch your step; Koko has started stealing banana peels."

Peggy was on her knees hugging the cats, who had come running.

Qwilleran thought, Those rascals! They know a pushover when they meet one; they're playing it to the hilt.

She declined a drink, saying she had to feed Dundee and then work at her computer.

Kenneth obviously wanted to stay. He said he could walk home.

"Agreeable young woman," Qwilleran said when she had driven away.

"She's nuts about cats," the young man said.

"Everyone's nuts about something. It's clear she's not local. What brought her here — do you know?"

"She's from Vegas. A fortune-teller told her to come here. She'd been through a nasty divorce. You know how she has all that hair covering her forehead? It covers a bad scar that she blames her ex-husband for."

"Well, I hope she's happy here. She seems to be an asset to the community. . . . Would you like to bring in the trunk?"

The contents were in good order. Kenneth had done fine work, and Qwilleran remunerated him, saying he'd enlist his services again. "How do you like your job at the *Something*? What brought you here in the first place? Not a fortune-teller, I imagine."

The young man showed signs of wanting to talk but feared he should not. His eyes darted.

Qwilleran knew to keep silent and look sympathetic; something about his brooding gaze and drooping moustache inspired confidence.

"I've got a suspect under surveillance," Kenneth said abruptly.

His listener raised a hand. "Say no more. I understand." He understood only that this was a copyboy playing at being an investigator — or an investigator disguised as a copyboy. Either way, it would be unfair to spoil his game. Remembering Kenneth's interest in *City of Brotherly Crime*, he assumed he was a copyboy pretending to be undercover — just as Celia Robinson operated as a secret agent when she first came to Moose County.

It was almost eleven p.m. when the phone rang. Qwilleran was reading a bedtime story to the Siamese and he switched voices hopefully to the mellifluous "good evening" that had given Polly a frisson of pleasure in the past, B.P.C. (Before Pirate's Chest).

"Qwill, you old geezer!" came the strident tones that he knew well.

"Lyle, you old dunderhead! You got back live from Saint Paul!"

"I've been back for a week — in time for all the hoopla downtown. Lisa was riding high until the news broke about the theft. What's your take on that little matter?"

"I agree with the police that it's an opportunist from Down Below. Tell Lisa: The good news is that the extra publicity will probably sell all the books in the jelly cupboard."

"You always were a confounded optimist, Qwill! . . . Are you in good voice for tomorrow night?"

"Have no fear about the speaker, Lyle. Worry whether we'll have an audience, considering that we're not serving refreshments."

To take his mind off the Edd Smith saga that had filled his head for the last forty-eight hours, Qwilleran selected a book from his journalism library that Violet Hibbard had wanted to give him. It brought to mind that their first spirited dinner date would not be repeated. He had begun to see her as a successor to the longtime dining companion that he seemed to be losing. It was the quality and subject matter of the conversation that had made both women interesting.

Both Qwilleran and the retired professor liked Shakespeare, and he would be willing to give Lord Byron an educated try. But now the lady had acquired a husband. Was it Judd, the retired engineer at the guest house? He was the right age, and only a short meeting had proved him to be congenial and talkative — though probably not about sonnets and Russian plays.

Polly had spoiled him in that respect; she could happily spend a half hour discussing the meaning of a single word.

SIXTEEN

On the morning of the lit club debut, Qwilleran met Alden Wade at the bookstore to discuss arrangements. Two of the lower-level meeting rooms would be thrown into one to accommodate fifty chairs, with a center aisle for projection equipment.

At the front of the room would be a low platform and a lectern and a row of three potted plants sent to the bookstore by well-wishers. Behind the speaker, a plain white wall would make a scene for the slides — not as a picture show but as pictorial atmosphere. John Bushland would come in to test the facilities in advance.

"About timing," Alden said. "The doors open at seven-thirty. The business meeting starts at eight with election of officers."

"What time do you want me to report?"

"Between eight and eight-thirty. Use your key and come in the side door. Stay in the office with Dundee until we're ready to introduce you."

"Does Dundee make his entrance with

me?" Qwilleran asked.

"Dundee stays in the office all evening. He's too much of a scene stealer. Any questions?"

"What to wear?"

"I'd say . . . jacket, no tie. And by the way, the parking lots at north and south ends will both be full, but there'll be a space reserved at the side door for you."

Qwilleran found it a pleasure to do business with Alden; he was always so well organized.

At the barn, Koko's frantic cavorting in the kitchen window brought Qwilleran indoors on the double. Strangely, the phone had not started to ring. Stranger still, when it did ring, it was an unusual call from Moira MacDiarmid.

"Qwill, I need to discuss something with you. Is this a suitable time?"

"There's nobody here but two nosy cats, and they can be trusted. What is it, Moira?"

"I know Kip and I talked about having dinner with you and Polly soon, but my husband abhors gossip, and this is rather . . . speculative."

Qwilleran's curiosity was piqued. Although not prone to spread gossip, he was

186

willing to listen to it, especially when it was called "speculation." What his friend's wife was suggesting was a private conference — not easy to do in either Lockmaster or Pickax without arousing suspicion. He got the message.

"Are you there, Qwill?"

"I'm here. I'm thinking. I need a topic for Tuesday's column, and — since Dundee has been such a hit in these parts — a dissertation on the marmalade breed would be of great interest to my readers. Since you're the sole authority on the subject, an interview with you would be expedient. Could you spare time tomorrow afternoon?"

"Oh, Qwill!"

"How many residents do you have in your cattery at the moment? Could they be available for interviewing tomorrow afternoon at one-thirty?"

After a few guarded words on Moira's part and a few noncommittal words on Qwilleran's, they hung up. He was chuckling to himself; there was nothing like a little intrigue to add zip to the daily routine. As for Koko, he was sitting on the kitchen counter, listening. How had he known the phone was going to ring? How had he known the caller was a cat breeder in the next county?

Koko jumped off the counter and went under the kitchen table, where he stared at his empty plate. Qwilleran gave him a morsel of Gouda cheese and had a slice of it himself.

That was the evening that fifty good folk of Moose County met at The Pirate's Chest to found the Pickax Literary Club. They elected Lyle Compton president, Mavis Adams vice president, Jill Handley secretary, Gordie Shaw treasurer, and Alden Wade program chairman.

The keynote speaker, sporting a green blazer and trimmed moustache, drove to the bookstore, found his reserved parking space, and let himself in the side door. Peggy was feeding the cat.

"Dundee is dining fashionably late this evening," Qwilleran said.

"I'm running behind schedule with my work, but he doesn't mind," she said. "Why are you sneaking in the back door, Mr. Q? You're the star of the whole show!"

"I was told to report here and stay out of sight until called to the platform. . . . And by the way, would your overworked computer be able to do a little research for the 'Qwill Pen'?"

"Love to! Sit down and tell me about it."

"Did you see the dedication of the bookstore? There was some ruckus about ribbon cutting. How did the custom originate? When? Where? Why? I need it early next week."

At that moment there was a knock on the door, and Qwilleran followed Alden to the meeting room.

"Stay outside the entrance, Qwill, until I give you a grand introduction — everything but the trumpets. Then burst through the door and go to the platform with a masterful stride. You know how to grab an audience!"

Qwilleran waited until he heard "James Mackintosh Qwilleran." He waited another three seconds, then entered briskly, throwing the salute that downtown pedestrians knew so well. All fifty of them rose to their feet in a torrent of applause.

After all, he was more than a popular columnist and a sympathetic listener to anyone with a problem. He was the modest presence behind the K Fund and everything it had done for the county.

He nodded graciously and used two hands, palms down, to coax them back into their seats.

The lights dimmed, except for one soft downlight over speaker and lectern. On the back wall appeared a blowup of an old gray-on-gray photo; a frail little man in front of a little old bookshop.

"Ladies and gentlemen, we would not be here tonight, launching a literary club under the auspices of a first-class bookstore, if it were not for the late Eddington Smith."

(More applause)

"For fifty years he sold pre-owned books in the quaint old shop where this building now stands. Before that his father peddled books from door to door, and Eddington went along as a willing helper when he didn't have to go to school."

Visual: Father and son standing alongside a horse-drawn van: "Smith Book Wagon."

"The books were sold on credit: Ten cents down and the rest later. Eddington told me that none of their charge customers ever defaulted.

"Did you ever think that Eddington was a rather elegant name for the modest Edd that we knew? It was his mother's maiden name. She taught school in the days of one-room schoolhouses."

Visual: Severe-faced woman in high-necked blouse, holding book and ruler.

"The ruler, we presume, was for rapping the knuckles of slow students. Edd always spoke fondly of his father but never mentioned his mother. Perhaps his knuckles had been rapped once too often."

(Laughter)

"But before the stern mother and book-loving father . . . there was Eddington's grandfather."

Visual: Old oak tree.

"And thereby hangs a tale.

"Upon the formation of Moose County, the founding fathers needed to establish a county seat, centrally located. And there — where two trails intersected in the wilderness — they found a rusty pickax in a tree stump. It was an omen! A backwoods building boom commenced overnight, and a local blacksmith was kept busy producing nails to build homes and shops. Then he was kicked in the head by a horse! No blacksmith . . . no nails!

"At the height of the panic, a stalwart young man walked into town and said he was a blacksmith.

" 'Can you make nails?' he was asked.

" 'Of course I can make nails.'

" 'What's your name?'

" 'John.'

" 'John what?'

"The cocky young man said, 'That's all the name you need to make nails.'

"It was highly irregular, but they needed nails, so his name was put on the town rolls as John B. Smith, the initial standing for 'Black.'

"John was a tall, brawny fellow. To quote the poet: 'He had large and sinewy hands and muscles like iron bands.' All the young women were after him, it was said, but the one he married was considered the best catch. Not only could she cook and sew but she could read and write — skills that were scarce among the early settlers.

"John built a home for his family, using feldspar, a stone that sparkled in the sunlight. He built it with his own hands. In the backyard was a mighty oak tree, and under its spreading branches he set up his anvil.

"The oak tree has long gone. Either it succumbed to old age and heavy rains . . . or Edd had it removed to make room for more parking spaces that he could rent to downtown workers.

"Edd, for all his shyness, was a practical man. He first acquired a cat to discourage the mice that were nibbling on the books. But a succession of Winstons became an attraction for tourists and local shoppers alike. By now, everyone knows that the cat's famous namesake was an American author and not a British prime minister."

Visual: Winston, dusting books with his tail.

"The presence of a live-in cat was not entirely responsible for the food odors that mingled with the mustiness of old books. Besides Winston's sardines, there were Edd's favorites — liver and onions, canned clam chowder, and garlic potatoes."

(Chuckles)

"There was a rickety wooden ladder, eight feet high — used by Edd for stocking shelves and by Winston for surveying noisy schoolchildren, and by the book scouts from Down Below, looking for two-dollar books worth a hundred in the rare-book market.

"Edd liked to tease the scouts. If I happened to be present he would tell outrageous lies about fabulous discoveries made on the upper shelves, and the book scout would almost fall off the ladder."

(Ripple of amusement)

"Edd himself was not a reader, yet he quoted frequently from the great writers of the past. He confessed to me that he had taken the advice of a great British statesman: 'If a man is not educated, he should own a book of quotations.' "

(Amused murmur)

"He also repaired books for schools, public libraries, and private collections, and his bookbinding equipment was in the back room of the shop — along with his sleeping cot, a two-burner hot plate, and a portable ice chest.

"There was a cracked mirror above a rusty old sink, and a shelf with old-fashioned shaving tackle along with a handgun. Later in life he said he was glad he never had to use the handgun because . . . he never had any bullets."

(Laughter)

"Was that a serious sentiment from a little old man? Or was it an example of pioneer humor? Edd, being descended from pioneers, had inherited their style of humor, although he was not a jokester like the country folk who keep everyone laughing in the coffee shops.

"Edd and I had a few adventures together. On one occasion we were threatened by an intruder intent on murder. I managed to subdue him, and I shouted to Edd, 'Call the police!' In a hesitant voice he asked, 'What shall I tell them?' "

(Laughter)

"On one of my visits to the bookstore, Edd told me some good news: The

Boosters Club was naming him Merchant of the Year! 'I can hardly wait to tell my father!' he said.

"I looked at him curiously, because I was sure his father was deceased.

" 'I talk to him every night,' he explained.

" 'How long has he been gone?' I asked as calmly as I could.

" 'Fourteen years,' he replied. 'He has gone to a better land — far, far away.' And his sober face was suffused with quiet joy."

Visual: The images on the back wall began changing in slow, tantalizing succession, with emphases on the blacksmith's oak tree and the pirate's chest found during excavation for the new bookstore.

"Now, my friends, the scandalous rumor that John B. Smith — the blacksmith who made the nails that helped build Pickax — was a weekend pirate! Can we believe that this hardworking husband and father who took his family to church twice a week and built them a house with his own hands and visited his old mother frequently — can we believe he put a red bandanna on his head and a gold hoop in one ear and forced victims at dagger-point to walk the plank?

"True, there were pirates preying on shipping in the big lakes. True, Edd's grandfather failed to return from a trip 'to visit his old mother.' True, a 'pirate's chest' with iron straps was found under the big oak.

"But consider this: There were no banks in those days, and it was customary to bury one's money, usually behind the outhouse."

(Chuckles)

"It's quite likely that the blacksmith built sturdy chests and sold them for that purpose. It's quite likely that he did visit his elderly mother at intervals to fix her roof, plant a garden, and scrub the floors. It's likely that Edd Smith was listening to the delirious babbling of a dying woman when he heard the scandalous secret.

"I say the scandalous secret of the blacksmith's wife is pure myth. Does anyone agree with me? If so, will you please stand?"

The county historian was the first to rise, followed by all the officers of the club, the college president, the K Fund attorney, the editor of the newspaper, teachers, and everyone else in the audience.

The lights came up, and Qwilleran stepped down from the platform and shook hands with the audience as they filed out.

The last to leave was Polly. "Qwill! You were wonderful! I was so proud I couldn't keep back the tears! . . . If you say it's a myth, I believe it's a myth! I've missed you so much in the last few weeks. . . ."

"I've missed you, too, Polly. The eleven-o'clock phone calls . . . and the dinner dates with good conversation . . ."

"And the musicales afterward."

"I have a fabulous new recording of Tchaikovsky's Fifth. Would you like to come to the barn to hear it? I promise to get you home by a respectable hour."

"It doesn't have to be respectable to-night," she said. "Tomorrow is my day off."

SEVENTEEN

On Friday morning Qwilleran ate his cereal and sliced bananas without complaint, and he opened a festive can of cocktail shrimp for the cats. He and Polly were together again. They would be dining at the Grist Mill, listening to great music, having long discussions about words, phoning each other at eleven p.m.

At the barn, following the lit club meeting, there had not been a single word about the Book Log Computer System! And Qwilleran had given her the blue cashmere robe that celebrated her matriculation from public library to bookstore.

Now he wanted to close the barn for the winter and move to Indian Village. Unit Number Four at the Willows would be readied by Pat O'Dell's janitorial service and "fluffed up" by the "be-whiching" Mrs. Fulgrove.

 Qwilleran walked with a light step to the newspaper office to file his Friday column before the noon deadline and then back downtown for lunch at the Mackintosh Inn. On the way he passed the Sprenkle Building, and a young man rushed out from the Wix & Wix Realty office, saying, "Mr. Q! Mr. Q! I have that book for you. Can you pop in for a minute?"

He was one of the duck hunters at the Hibbard Guest House who had invited him out for a weekend shoot.

"I'm a washout with a rifle," he had told them, "but I'd be interested in duck habitat as a topic for the 'Qwill Pen.'"

"We've got a book at the office you can borrow," the younger Wix had said. "We'll dig it out."

So now he had drifted in, and they had dug out their copy of the duck book.

"Pleasant office," Qwilleran said. "Are you brothers? Is Wix a local family?"

"It's really W-I-C-K-E-S, but Bud and I decided the short spelling would be more eye-catching on a sign and easier for the public to remember. Alden has been telling us about your barn. If you ever want to unload it, Wix and Wix would like to list it."

"Take a number," Qwilleran said genially.

"Alden's a terrific guy! Not only is he a terrific shot with a duck rifle, he can play the piano. He can act. He can sing. The gals are wild about him. He's a good organizer. He has ideas. . . . How's the Hibbard book coming?"

"It's been photographed, and I'm collecting material for the text. Do you have any stories to add?"

"Only what we talk about when we're out on the boat — just brainstorming, you know: Violet could develop her thirty acres if and when she gets tired of being a landlady. The house could be made into a spa — with upscale condos and apartments all around."

"No shopping mall, I hope," Qwilleran said with veiled sarcasm.

"No, but there'd be room for one or two good restaurants."

Qwilleran stood up. "Thanks for the book. I'll return it. Sorry to dash off. I've got an appointment in Lockmaster."

In the early afternoon Qwilleran drove to Lockmaster for some grist for the "Qwill Pen" mill . . . and some *speculation*.

Moira MacDiarmid was ready for him with coffee and bite-size marmalade tartlets.

"How's our little sweetheart?" she asked.

"Presuming that you mean Dundee, he's happily basking in an effulgence of compliments. Do you have some good information on the breed? Prior to the reign of Dundee the First, my only acquaintance with a reddish cat was on Goodwinter Boulevard, where we were house-sitting one year. He was dirty-orange, fat as a pig, and with foul breath. He kept coming to our back door and annoying the Siamese."

Moira said, "Some ginger cats are enormous, and their owners boast about their weight. We breed our marmalades for a modern taste. Gingers can be tiger-striped, splotched, or all one shade in a choice of spicy colors; our marmalades are apricot and cream in a nonthreatening stripe. . . . But did you know Sir Winston Churchill always had a 'ginger tom' in his home? And his will specified that there always be a ginger tom in residence at Chartwell, his estate."

Qwilleran asked for names and phone numbers of marmalade fanciers who would be willing to be interviewed. And that was that! The conversation shifted to . . . speculation.

Qwilleran said, "You had something interesting on your mind when you called me."

"Yes. Kathie wanted me to talk to you. When you so kindly let us into the bookstore and bought us ice cream in that delightful little shop, there was a young man there who Kathie thought she recognized. Though he had a beard, she thought he was her old boyfriend Wesley. But you said his name was Kenneth and he was a copyboy at the *Something*. There was no time to argue; she had to catch a plane."

"Does she have a special interest in Wesley, aka Kenneth?"

"Nothing serious," Moira said, "but they've known each other all through high school and enrolled in J school at the state university at the same time. Then Wesley never showed up for classes, and it worried her. He simply disappeared."

"How about his parents? Are they worried?"

"They're both deceased. Kip knew Wesley's father. Kip said he was a high roller in the stock market and lost everything. He shot himself, but I think there was more to the story than that." She stopped abruptly and looked wise. "I think his wife was cheating on him; he was a very proud type. And . . . after his suicide, his wife remarried too soon — much too soon!"

"Classical situation," Qwilleran murmured. "Straight out of Shakespeare."

"Kathie says Wesley adored his father and hated his stepfather. He kept his father's surname. . . . I'm babbling on and forgetting my manners. Will you have more coffee, Qwill?"

He nodded. She poured and went on: "Kathie is afraid Wesley will follow his father's example. . . . But Kip made a discreet inquiry at the bank and discovered that withdrawals were still being made from Wesley's trust fund . . . so you can see how badly Kathie wanted your Kenneth to be our Wesley-with-beard."

Qwill said, "Tell Kathie that Kenneth is doing some research for me, and I may be able to do a little undercover investigating."

On the drive to Pickax, Qwilleran reflected on how much had happened since his previous drive with Dundee in a coop beside him. And he thought how relieved he would be to close the barn and move to Indian Village for the winter. There would be less distraction, and he could work on the Hibbard House book, he would be a few doors away from Polly, the batty Wetherby Goode, and — now — even the cats' veterinarian! How would the cats react to Dr. Constable as a neighbor, dropping in for coffee? Yum Yum would run and hide under the bed; Koko would greet her with throaty purrs, thinking she had brought her thermometer.

Qwilleran's amusement at the possibility was interrupted by a phone call; he pulled off the road.

It was Janice on the line. "Qwill, Bushy said it was all right to call on your cell phone. Have you seen today's paper?"

"No. I've been interviewing in Lockmaster for the 'Qwill Pen.' What's the news I've missed?"

"The wedding announcement. Violet has married Alden Wade!"

"Is that so? I thought it would be that white-haired engineer. It would be handy to have an engineer in the family."

"Yes, I thought they were a cute couple, too."

"How did Bushy react?"

"He says Alden is . . . all wrong for Violet!"

That was all Janice cared to say on the phone, and Qwilleran drove the rest of the way home in a state of fascinated . . . speculation. What would Polly say? Maggie? Lisa? Wetherby? And, for that matter, Koko?

★ ★ ★

Toward dinnertime, Qwilleran drove out Ittibittiwassee Road to Indian Village to pick up Polly in Unit One of the Willows. There were signs that the doctor was already in Unit Two. The occupant of Number Three would be at Station WPKX at this hour, bamboozling his listeners about the weather, as Qwilleran took pleasure in telling him.

He used his key to unlock Polly's door but also gave the doorbell their secret code-ring, the first four notes (approximately) of Beethoven's Fifth.

Brutus and Catta came running to meet him, followed by Polly in her plum-colored suit with pink blouse and opal earrings, and she had been to the hairdresser. Qwilleran was wearing coordinated grays blending with his graying hair, gray eyes, and pepper-and-salt moustache.

"See? The little dears are happy to see you!"

"They're happy because they know I'm not staying long," he said.

As they drove away, Polly remarked, "Dr. Constable's furniture arrived today. It's been in storage pending the final divorce settlement. She's been eager to get away from the guest house. She said the mood changed after Alden moved in."

"From what — to what?"

"She said the relaxed family feeling changed to a formal, terribly proper atmosphere. . . . I know you won't mention this."

"Did you see the wedding announcements in today's paper, Polly?"

"No, but several people phoned me. What motivated her? Love? Loneliness? Some practical consideration? Women find him very attractive. But — I hesitate to say this — my assistant, who's from Lockmaster, says he has a reputation as a fortune hunter."

A negative thought entered Qwilleran's mind, but he squelched it. He said, "Violet seems in a hurry to have the Hibbard book published, as if she's afraid the house will burn down. Bushy has photographed it inside and out, so . . . Anyway, all I have to do now is tell the Hibbard story in beautiful prose."

His arch remark was taken seriously by Polly, who admired his writing.

At the Grist Mill there were admiring glances from other diners and a questioning look from Derek Cuttlebrink. He seated them under the murderous scythe on the wall, saying, "I just found out it's

206

made of plastic. If it falls off the wall it might splash your soup, but it won't decapitate anybody."

"*Bon appetit*," Qwilleran said.

When the waiter took their order, it was Chicken Venezia for her and Sirloin Marsala for him.

Conversation at the table was about . . . words.

How Bill Turmeric had explained Mrs. Fulgrove's use of "which."

How Koko was fascinated by George Ade's *Fables in Slang* simply because it was a small book.

How Violet had used the word "repair" correctly when most people would say "retire."

For dessert they had plum buckle.

EIGHTEEN

There were no crowds on Saturday morning. No cheers. No band music. No TV cameras. There was only Roger MacGillivray, weekend photographer-reporter for the *Something*, to cover the event. The K Theatre was being renamed Theatre Arts.

Large block letters had been cut from aluminum and then mounted directly on the fieldstone building with a little space between.

The style had originated with the Mackintosh Inn, suggested by K Fund designers. It was now becoming popular in the City of Stone. In this case, an element of mystery was created by doing the work under the cover of darkness and covering it with canvas until the official unveiling. Only Larry Lanspeak and Alden Wade were present to pose for pictures and give Roger a press release.

Qwilleran was the one invited spectator; after all, the name had been his idea. Roguishly he thought it would be a laugh if the workmen had made a typographical error — putting the A before the E, or the E before the R.

The new name marked the theatre club's new venture: a program of classes in acting technique, voice culture, stage makeup, and set-building, under the direction of Alden Wade.

Qwilleran wished them well, then rushed home to the barn to attend to his own program: moving his household to Indian Village for the winter . . . and writing a book on the historic Hibbard House. He needed to collect stories about "the big house on the hill" from people who had been there.

Once more he called upon Whiskers for legwork, although he had a private reason for wanting to speak with the young man.

The Siamese sensed that a friend was approaching through the woods, and they staged a welcoming demonstration in the kitchen window.

"What are they all excited about?" Kenneth asked when he walked in.

"You! Speak to them."

"Hello, cats."

Qwilleran said, "Sit at the snack bar. I've thawed some sweet rolls from Celia Robinson. I hope you like your coffee strong.

Do you know Celia Robinson? Remarkable woman. When I first moved up here and was doing a little private investigating, she was my undercover agent." He watched for Kenneth's reaction. It was sudden but guarded.

"Now about the Hibbard House: Your work with the documents was excellent. We need to collect personal memoirs from old-timers who visited the house and/or knew the family. Your first source: the historical collection at the public library. Next, call Thornton Haggis, the county historian, for names of members of the Old-Timers Club who are over eighty. I'll tell him to expect your call."

Kenneth was taking notes.

"I'm going to tell Thorn — that's what he likes to be called — that three hot subjects are better than a dozen warm bodies. I suggest you do the interviews on weekends. You'll need a car."

"I can borrow Peg's."

"No. Keep this on a professional basis. Rent a car and put it on your bill. I'll give you a pocket tape recorder for the interviews. Any questions?"

Kenneth asked intelligent ones. Then Qwilleran asked one of him: "Do you know a Kathie MacDiarmid in Lockmaster? She's in J school now. She and her mother came to visit Dundee last weekend. Dundee came from Mrs. MacDiarmid's cattery." The short sentences were intended to allow the young man to collect his wits before the Big One. "I took them to Granny's. You were there with Peggy. Kathie thought you were someone she knew."

"Yeah, we were in high school at the same time."

"But she thought your name was Wesley. I set her straight."

Kenneth took time to gulp and look from side to side before answering. "I had a family problem, sort of. I wanted to work for the *Something*, but I didn't want anyone to know I was here."

With sympathy in his voice and understanding in his brooding eyes, Qwilleran said, "I know how those things happen. If there's anything I can do to help, it's strictly confidential. Don't hesitate to ask."

There was a long, pathetic silence until Kenneth said abruptly, "What's he doing?"

Koko was butting Kenneth's ankles with the top of his head.

"Cats are smart. They know right from wrong. Koko has exceptional instincts in this regard. He knows the good guys from the bad guys. He approves of what you're doing. You don't have to explain."

Kenneth went on gulping, and Koko went on butting his ankles.

"I want to talk about it," he said. "My stepfather is living here. I don't think he's to be trusted. There's nothing I can do about it. I don't have any proof — any evidence against him. All I can do is watch him. It's not just the way kids have always hated their stepfathers. It's just that . . . I don't know . . . am I wrong?"

Qwilleran put his hand to his moustache. "I know what you mean. I have the same unexplainable reaction at times. I call it a hunch, and the strange thing is . . . the way it turns out, I'm always right. So what can I say? You have to play your hunches. Do what you're doing, but keep your eyes open and your mind alert. And if you want to talk about this again, you know you've got a sympathetic listener. Two listeners, including Koko."

Kenneth's visit had left Qwilleran with a feeling of satisfaction about the Hibbard research; he would call Thornton Haggis and alert him to the need for interviews with old-timers.

On the other hand, the young man's

emotional outpouring had left Qwilleran with a tingling sensation on his upper lip, and he found himself patting his moustache frequently. The wicked stepfather of fairy tales was obviously Alden Wade; Kenneth was obviously Wesley, whose father was a suicide and whose mother was the victim of a sniper's bullet.

Yet Alden Wade was lauded in Pickax for his charm, helpfulness, polished manners, and many skills. Qwilleran himself recognized his acting talent, fine voice, and well-organized mind. All the while, there were friends of Qwilleran's who called the newcomer a lady-killer, home breaker, and fortune hunter.

Qwilleran had two reasons to visit Maggie Sprenkle again, and he called to make an appointment. He would pick up his tape recorder with her memories of early days at the Hibbard House. And he would ask what she thought about Violet's sudden marriage.

On the phone, he asked casually if she had recalled any incidents from the good old days at Hibbard House.

"Yes, I have! And I was just thinking about you, Qwill. Would you care to come over for a cup of tea?"

He walked downtown — for the last time

until April — and soon he was sitting in the plush Victorian parlor, drinking jasmine tea and listening to Maggie's Hibbard House memories. He heard about a Fourth of July bonfire that got out of hand and terrified everyone . . . a black bear that came to the back door and terrified the cook . . . a berry-picking party that got lost in the thirty-acre woods.

Qwilleran said, "You've got the right idea, Maggie. Don't stop thinking. I'm moving to the Village for the winter and plan to start writing, but first I have to visualize the whole book and what I can do to make it distinctive." He drained his teacup and stood up.

"Wait a minute! Sit down!" she said.

He sat down.

"What do you think about Violet's sudden marriage, Qwill?"

"What can I say? Love is like lightning. It can strike anywhere."

"You're being polite. You know this was a marriage of convenience! Violet is twenty years his senior and extremely wealthy! And I told you about her health problem. Lately she's been having headaches and touches of numbness that worry me. I'm sure they worry her, too, although she's careful not to show it. I know her, Qwill!

When we were growing up, we were like sisters. We're still close friends. Why didn't she tell me about her intentions! Did she think I'd try to stop her? . . . What do you know about Alden Wade, Qwill?"

"Only that he has many talents and a pleasing personality —"

"And a taste for older women with money!"

In a flash, Qwilleran remembered Janice's confidential gossip that the marriage announcement was being delayed until Violet could change her will. He also remembered the realty man's dream of "developing" the Hibbard property.

Maggie had stopped for breath; her face was reddening.

"Calm down, Maggie. Take a deep breath. Violet is an intelligent woman, and she must know what she's doing. Who's her attorney? She must be getting good advice."

"The family always retained the Hasselrich people. After the old man died, I'm sure she stayed with the firm."

"They're highly reputable. They wouldn't let Violet do anything foolish."

"I'm sorry, Qwill. Excuse my outburst. It's just that . . . I haven't had anyone to talk to."

"I understand perfectly. And the K Fund has a stake in the future of Hibbard House now. I'll draw it to their attention. Has Violet been in touch with you since the Friday announcement?"

"No. I tried to call her. I think she's avoiding me."

"It's been only forty-eight hours."

"You're right, Qwill. You've said exactly what Jeremy would have said if he were here."

That evening, when Qwilleran and Polly drove to the Boulder House Inn on the lakeshore, it was their first genuine Saturday-night dinner date in a long time. There was no mention of the Book Log Computer System.

"How's Dundee?" Qwilleran asked.

"Oh, he's so happy! Not frisky — just happily interested in whatever is happening in the store. You know the table where we feature the book of the week? Well, recently we did a table on *A Place Called Happiness*, and Dundee jumped up and presided over it like an author waiting to 'pawtograph' his books."

"Who wrote it?"

"A psychologist, Dr. Dori Seider. It's selling very well and is up for discussion at the next meeting of the lit club. One of the Green Smocks thinks we should send a copy, anonymously, to our cranky mayor."

"Amanda wouldn't read it," Qwilleran said. "She'd throw it at the messenger."

"Dr. Seider has two cats, you'll be glad to know. I have an autographed book that you can borrow, Qwill. She quotes John Milton's *Paradise Lost*: 'The mind is its own place, and in itself can make a Heaven of Hell, a Hell of Heaven.' What do you think of that?"

Qwilleran later recorded the rest of the evening in his personal journal.

Saturday, October 4 — There's something magical about the Boulder House: the lake view, walking on the beach, the sky full of sunset, Squunk cocktails on the parapet. Not to mention Rocky, the cat, who always greets us with ankle rubbing, a high compliment.

Polly's soft voice and musical laugh have returned. First I gave her a limerick I wrote a few weeks ago, when her sense of humor was below par:

A literacy maven named Polly
Says slang expressions are folly.

She refuses to say
"Drop dead!" or "No way!"
Or "Dingbat" or "Oops!" or "By golly!"

Then I gave her a brilliant new recording of Saint-Saëns's *Third Symphony,* and we went to the barn and listened to it.

NINETEEN

 On Sunday afternoon Qwilleran and two nervous Siamese would leave for their winter address. The more the departure was delayed, he had learned, the more nervous they became, as if they feared they would be left behind!

Moving fifteen miles away to Indian Village was no easier than moving fifteen thousand. Friends, neighbors, and business connections had to be notified.

Chief Brodie always volunteered to keep an eye on the property. Mrs. Fulgrove would come in and empty the refrigerator, taking home any food she might be able to use; a few frozen desserts were purchased and added to the freezer to make it worth her while. And Pat O'Dell's crew would secure the premises against the winter weather.

Before leaving town, Qwilleran wanted to take one last walk through the woods and around Winston Park.

Walking back to the barn, Qwilleran realized that it would be the last of these pleasurable strolls for six months: Emerging from the patch of dense woods into the barnyard, checking the kitchen window for the welcoming committee, unlocking the door, being surrounded by waving tails . . . how could he describe the good feeling he experienced?

On this Sunday afternoon there was only one cat signaling from the window, indicating a message on the machine. Wetherby Goode wanted him to call. First, though, he had to phone his attorney — at home.

"Sorry to bother you on Sunday, Bart."

"No bother. It's a pleasure. Our office got the message that you're moving to the Village today."

"Yes, and I wonder if you would stop at my condo on your way into town tomorrow morning. I have something quite interesting to discuss. Same condo — Unit Four in the Willows."

Then Qwilleran phoned Unit Three. "Joe, we're leaving for the Village. What's up?"

"Dr. Connie is now in Unit Two. The Willows has a full house again. How'll it be if you all shuffle over to my place for a pizza supper? Polly will do the salad.

Linguini's will deliver pizza and spumone, and we'll have beer, wine, and Squunk water for the Squunks."

"Okay with me! Is there anything I can contribute?"

"You might sing a song. I'll play the piano."

The Siamese had spent several winters in the condo, but when they emerged from their travel coop, everything was new and strange. Even the fresh water in their drinking bowl was suspect — and the shag rug in front of the fireplace — and the plates on which their dinner was served. But by the time Qwilleran returned from the pizza party, they would be chasing each other up and down the stairs, rolling voluptuously on the shag rug, and burrowing behind the sofa pillows, looking for last winter's treasures.

Meanwhile, Qwilleran changed into something that would impress his host and evoke the admiration of Polly and Dr. Constable.

At Unit Three, Qwilleran was greeted by Jet Stream, a husky tiger as extroverted as the man he lived with.

To the veterinarian he said, "Dr. Constable! What lured you away from Hibbard House?"

"Call me Connie," she said. "Well, you see, my divorce just became final, and I wanted to start a new lifestyle. I want to be able to cook and have pets and entertain guests. How are Koko and Yum Yum?"

"They're glad to have their favorite doctor in the neighborhood. Is it the blue coat you wear? Everyone else at the clinic wears white."

"This is not for publication," said Connie, who was wearing blue denims. "I wear blue to make my eyes look blue."

"But it's true that cats respond to blue. Yellow and blue are the colors they see best, although they live in a world of fuzzy pastels."

They went on at some length about the vision of cats until Wetherby interrupted.

"Are you two guys plotting to rob a bank? The pizza's here! Come and get it while it's hot!"

As they walked toward the dining area, Qwilleran said to Connie, "As you know, I'm writing a book about Hibbard House. If you hear any tales about the old landmark that I can use or even if I can't — please let me know."

At the table, the host said, "Connie, you're lucky to be arriving at this time. Now that the K Fund masterminds the

Village, the roof doesn't leak, the windows don't rattle, the floors don't bounce, and the walls between units are soundproofed. We're entering our Civilized Period."

Polly said, "There's a bird club that meets at the clubhouse once a week, and the path along the riverbank is ideal for birding. There's also a bridge club and an art club."

Qwilleran added, "And they keep the roads snowplowed and the walks shoveled. Linguini's and Tipsy's Tavern are nearby. In fact, we're close to the Hummocks and not far from Hibbard House."

Wetherby said, "And the view of the riverbank is super. Ask Jet Stream. . . . Ask Brutus and Catta. . . . Ask Koko and Yum Yum."

Later, when they moved to the living room for coffee, he added, "And now Qwill is going to sing a song."

"Sorry, I left my music at home. But I'll entertain you with a limerick about our congenial host."

He read from one of the index cards he always had in a jacket pocket:

A congenial fellow named Joe
Has learned how to make lots of dough
By forecasting weather

223

With salt and a feather,
But sometimes he has to eat crow.

Everyone laughed. Wetherby proposed a nightcap. Then they said goodnight, and Qwilleran accompanied the two women to their respective doors.

When he returned to Unit Four, he found two demanding cats and a message from Kenneth on the machine: "Mr. Q, I collected some good stuff. Want me to speed out to your place tomorrow night?"

Qwilleran called him and said, "Yes, I'd like to get an idea of the stories we can expect from the old-timers. If I order two dinners from Lois's, could you bring them out here? How does that sound?"

"I can handle that!" Kenneth said.

TWENTY

Facing east, the glass walls of the Willows provided not only a view of the riverbank but a warm morning sun that Koko and Yum Yum found ideal for washing up after breakfast. Qwilleran was basking in its warmth himself, with his second cup of coffee, when the attorney arrived.

"Nice place. Great view," he said as he dropped his briefcase on the coffee table.

Qwill said, "It may not give you the shot in the arm you get from the apple barn, Bart, but it should give you an environmental lift." The Barter family lived in the country, too, but among rolling hills and sheep farms. "Coffee?"

"By all means. And I picked up a couple of Danish at Tipsy's on the way here."

They sat at a small table in the window and Qwilleran asked, "Did you come via West Kennebeck? If so, you passed the Hibbard property."

"Yes, but it's heavily wooded. All you can see is the red roof and the tower.

How's the book faring?"

"I'm acquainting myself with the history of the family and house — and with Violet, the sole remaining heir. And that's why I called you. She's sixtyish, intelligent — obviously loaded — and with a life expectancy that's extremely iffy. And — without telling anyone — she has just married a younger man!"

"Maybe you should be writing a novel, Qwill. Who is he?"

"The actor you saw in the Oscar Wilde play, manager of special events at the bookstore, initiator of the theatre arts program to be announced in today's paper."

"Sure, I remember seeing him. He introduced you at the lit club debut. Talented guy — with a lot of polish. What's the problem? Jealousy? He's an outsider."

"The problem is, Bart, that in Lockmaster he has a reputation as a fortune hunter."

"*Hmff!* . . . The plot thickens!"

"She confided in another woman that she went to her attorney last Monday to have her will changed. One can only guess: How? I've talked to Violet and to her best friend, and both women have indicated that the preservation of Hibbard House is of greatest importance. And yet . . . This will sound, Bart, as if I've been playing private detective. There are realty professionals in town who dream of developing the Hibbard property as a big commercial venture."

"There's no law against dreaming, Qwill."

"Yes, but the Realtors are paying guests at Hibbard House and chummy with the new bridegroom. They go duck hunting together on weekends."

"All very interesting," the attorney said. "What do you want from me?"

"The Hibbards, according to Maggie Sprenkle, have always been clients of your firm. Since the K Fund is underwriting the book, it behooves us to inquire about the future of the building. Museum? School? Health spa? Gambling casino?"

"I see your point, Qwill."

"I don't want to know what the dear woman has written in her will. I simply want to know if the property is protected against commercial development. Otherwise, why should I waste my time on the book?"

"You're quite right, Qwill. How urgent is this matter?"

"Top priority! Her condition is precarious."

★ ★ ★

At the pizza party Connie had mentioned that she was taking a week off to get settled, and Qwilleran had mentioned that he needed to interview her about life in today's Hibbard House.

"Your place or my place?" she asked. "Mine is a mess."

On Monday afternoon she rang his doorbell, excusing her frazzled appearance but saying she needed to relax for a half hour.

He offered her coffee or a soft drink, and she chose the latter. "I've been warned about your coffee, Qwill. They say it's one degree short of illegal."

"Where would you like to sit?" he asked. "At the table in the window, or in one of the sofas where the cats hang out?"

"A sofa with cat hairs. I'm exhausted!"

Qwilleran served the drink, placed a tape recorder on the coffee table, and said, "How does the hoary old mansion adapt to modern living?"

"Well, on the second floor there are four large bedrooms with high ceilings and canopy beds. Each has its own sitting room and luxurious bath in what was called the 'water closet' in the days before indoor plumbing. The second generation of Hibbards did a lot of entertaining, and guests stayed a week or a month. It's like living in a movie set — fun for a year or so but not the kind of place where you'd like to spend the rest of your life. Actually, the other two women are also leaving. The one who's a hospital supervisor is taking a position in Rochester, and the one who's a teacher is getting married."

Qwilleran said, "Then there will be only male guests?"

"They say there's a waiting list for accommodations, but temporarily it will be strictly stag. The men's quarters are in the old guest house a hundred yards behind the main building. I've never been invited to one of their slosh parties, but you might talk to the Wix brothers or Judd Amhurst. Judd is very nice. Frankly, we thought Violet should have married him. But he has family in Texas, and they want him to move down there to be with his grandchildren."

With questioning, Connie told about a twenty-foot Christmas tree in the foyer one year . . . picnic suppers on the veranda in summer with deer coming to the porch for a handout . . . bridge and Ping-Pong tournaments . . . and, after Alden's arrival, dramatic readings in the library and classical concerts in the music room.

With amusement Qwilleran thought of the duck-hunting Wix brothers sitting still for a dramatic reading. . . . "Did everyone participate willingly in every activity?" he asked.

Connie thought a moment. "While Violet was house mother, we all went along with everything she suggested. She's such a gracious hostess, you know. But after Alden joined our happy family, nothing was quite the same. Violet was highly impressed with his sophistication and allowed him to call the plays. . . . Should I be telling you all these family secrets, Qwill?"

"I'll use discretion," he assured her.

Then he added, with the confidential tone that had melted icebergs, "Off the record, was Violet's marriage well received?"

Frowning, Connie said, "Not exactly. I don't know about the men, but to the girls it seemed like a bad choice. Don't ask me why. It's just a feeling. . . ."

At six o'clock Kenneth arrived in his rental car, carrying two dinner boxes from Lois's, and was greeted by Qwilleran and two eager Siamese.

"Wait'll you hear what I've got!" he said, patting the recording kit.

"Come in! We'll listen while the food's

230

reheating. Sit over there." Qwilleran indicated two cushiony sofas facing each other across the lush shag rug. It was clearly handmade, a wild tangle of long pile.

"Some rug!" Kenneth said.

"The cats think so, too."

Qwilleran served Q cocktails, and they listened to a male voice — not old, not young — telling the following tale:

My name is Henry Newsome, retired painter and paper hanger. I never worked on the Hibbard House. They always hired those high-priced decorators from Down Below. But when I was growing up, my mother talked about it. She'd been a live-in maid-of-all-work when she was a young girl. That would be almost a hundred years ago. I'm eighty. Her name was Lavinia, and that's what I'll call her.
(Slight cough)

Excuse me. It's just an allergy. Now, Mr. MacMurchy says you're interested in stories about that big old barn. No disrespect intended. My mother used to tell one story that would make a good movie. That's what we thought when we were kids. Anyway, here goes:

Mr. Geoffrey was master of the house

231

back then; that's what they were called then. Lavinia said he was a nice man. The mistress was kind of hard to please. They had one daughter, and she was a problem. In those days she was just called a bad girl. She ran off with a man to Milwaukee, or someplace like that. No one was allowed to speak her name.

(Cough)

Well, he turned out to be a wife beater, and she came back to Hibbard House with her baby. Of course, she was in the doghouse. Her mother kept saying, "I told you so!" Lavinia felt sorry for her.

(Cough)

One of Lavinia's jobs was to give the baby some fresh air, weather permitting. They had a real fancy baby carriage, and she wheeled it around and around the dirt roads on the property. There was no pavement in those days. Automobiles were just coming in. The Hibbards had one — all open, with side curtains.

One day Lavinia was pushing the carriage when suddenly an automobile came up alongside. Almost frightened her to death. There were two men in it, and one jumped out and grabbed the baby! Then they took off in a cloud of dust! Lavinia went screaming into the house. "They stole the baby! They stole the baby!" She thought it was her fault, and she was so sick, they put her to bed. Mrs. Hibbard said to her disgraced daughter, "I told you so!" And the poor girl went out to a pond on the property and drowned herself.

(Cough)

Lavinia didn't want to work there anymore, so she left, but she told us that no one knew what happened to the baby, and no one tried to find out.

"Good story, Ken! Get a few more as good as that, and we'll list you as assistant editor."

"You mean that? Mr. Haggis steered me to another story — how Hibbard House survived the worst snowstorm of the century, before snowplows and telephones and radio. There's a woman at the Senior Care Facility whose grandmother worked for the Hibbards. I thought I'd go to see her tomorrow after work, but visitors aren't allowed in the evening. So I asked the boss if I could get a couple of hours off — after the paper's put to bed, you know. I told him it was for you. He said okay."

They had dinner at the small table in the window, and the cats hung around.

Qwilleran explained, "They're not begging — just being sociable."

The two men chewed in friendly silence for a while, and then Kenneth asked, "Who else lives in this row?"

"Mrs. Duncan from the bookstore, a doctor from the pet clinic, and the weatherman."

"Wetherby Goode? He's crazy!"

"He's from Horseradish, and they're all slightly crazy! He has a cat named Jet Stream, a name that's appropriate for more reasons than one. . . . Speaking of Horseradish, the last remaining Hibbard has just married a native of that town. It was announced in Friday's paper. Everyone's talking about it."

Qwilleran paused, sensing a change in his guest's genial mood. Then he continued. "He's a lot younger than she is — and talented and personable, so he's considered quite a catch. But she's the sole heir to the Hibbard fortune — charming and intelligent — so she's a pretty good catch, too . . . especially since she's not in the best of health. Everyone is puzzling over their respective motives."

It was the kind of gossip that Qwilleran used to enjoy at the Press Club, where rumors and impolite facts were exchanged freely.

Kenneth had stopped eating. His face was reddening. Finally he interrupted. "He's my stepfather."

"Is that so?" Qwilleran feigned surprise, although he had guessed as much. "Then his previous wife, who was killed by a sniper, was your mother!"

In a choked voice Kenneth said, "She married him right after my father died. A lot of people in Lockmaster raised their eyebrows. And then, in a couple of years, she was killed by a sniper while riding her horse on a country trail. The sniper was never apprehended. So you know what people were saying!

"My stepfather is a duck hunter, and he has all kinds of guns, including a Remington 'Thirty Aught Six,' which would be good for a sniper."

"How about the official investigation?"

"Insufficient evidence. That's why I went to a police academy out west instead of J school."

"I can understand your feelings." It was said in the deeply sympathetic tone that brought forth confidences, confessions, and sometimes just tears. Kenneth jumped up and started walking around the room with his hands in his hip pockets.

"Shall we have some dessert?" Qwilleran asked.

"Thanks, but I've gotta get home."

Qwilleran said, "Anything that's said within these walls goes no further, Ken."

The boy left, and the Siamese followed him to the door. They had been listening.

Qwilleran spent the afternoon making something out of nothing — his way of referring to the "Qwill Pen." The duck hunting book lent to him by the Wix brothers would be the inspiration, and a column on duck habitat would be appropriate during "Duck Season," as the hunters called it. The problem was that the book — filled with gorgeous color photographs — was all about hunting, as its title implied. And hunting was not one of Qwilleran's many interests.

When the Wix brothers had invited him to join one of their shoots, he had said, "I'm a washout with a rifle." It was a fib. In his earlier days he had won Kewpie dolls at carnivals for shooting BBs at moving targets, and his marksmanship was much admired by the girls to whom he gave his prizes.

He had been born and bred in a metropolitan area where wildlife was for viewing in a zoo, not for shooting. He could not see himself pointing a gun at a furred or feathered creature.

As for ducks, he remembered the friendly brood that visited him daily when he was vacationing at Black Creek.

Ducks and ducklings skimmed across the quiet water without making a ripple or a splash. He could not imagine taking them home for dinner.

The book told him more than he wanted to know about "waterfowling" — guns, camouflage jackets, waders, duck blinds, and decoys. He learned that a drake is a male duck, and the female is a hen . . . that the daily bag limit allows for more drakes than hens . . . that there were divers, fishers, puddlers, and tree ducks. Species that sounded familiar were the mallards, mergansers, pintails, ring-necks, and buffleheads.

The book was informative as well as handsome, but it told him more than he needed to know — for the "Qwill Pen."

TWENTY-ONE

 Qwilleran filed his Tuesday copy for the "Qwill Pen" by motorcycle messenger — to avoid running into Kenneth. There had been something embarrassing about his outburst the previous evening — his outpouring of family secrets and unthinkable suspicions. It was nothing that could be blamed on "too much to drink" because Qwilleran had served nothing stronger than Squunk water. Kenneth's facts or fancies had been building up over a period of time. They had been suppressed, one could imagine, until that moment when encouraged by sympathetic listening. It would be prudent to let the matter cool for a while.

He also gave the motorcycle messenger the duck hunting book to return to Wix & Wix Realty. The Tuesday "Qwill Pen" was all about ducks without a single word about duck hunting. No matter. The *Something* had an outdoor writer whose job was to address the subject of hunting.

All these thoughts were formulated and

decisions made while Qwilleran ate his cereal and sliced bananas. They were interrupted by a phone call from the attorney.

"Nothing to worry about, Qwill. The Hibbard House is legally protected. Full speed ahead!"

Even so, he felt uneasy and disorganized. He remembered his mother's philosophy: "When you don't know what to do with yourself, do something for someone else."

Qwilleran went to Unit Two and rang the doorbell. "Do you need anyone to do backbreaking labor without charge?" he asked. "I'm available. Offer good for today only."

"I do! I do!" Connie said. "How are you at unpacking books?"

There were twenty boxes and a whole wall of empty shelves. "It was the bookshelves that attracted me to this place," she said.

"A rare-book dealer lived here and had them built," Qwilleran explained. "He didn't stay long. He was an ailurophobe, and I think he was unnerved by the caterwauling coming from both sides. The walls have since been soundproofed. . . . Now, how do you want the books organized on the shelves?"

"In categories. Each box is labeled 'history,' 'biography,' or whatever. I'll be unpacking things in the kitchen."

"I see a lot of boxes marked 'science.' Is that veterinary science?"

"No. Those belonged to my father. He was a science teacher in high school, and his hobby was reading everything on any branch of science. I tried to get him interested in mystery novels for relaxation, but he said fiction was a waste of time."

Qwilleran enjoyed handling books and had to resist opening each one and reading a page, especially those with titles like *Quantum Control of Molecular Processes* and *Physical Properties of Carbon Nanotubes*.

When the job was finished and the empty boxes were carried down to the basement garage, he said to Connie, "Anytime you feel the need of a coffee break, I could offer you some of my notorious brew and some Scotch Danish. They're regular Danish rolls but smaller and cheaper. I'll start the coffee. You come over when you're ready."

When she arrived, she was wearing jeans and a gray sweatshirt and was appraised by Koko, as if he sensed her identity but questioned her credentials.

After they were seated at the snack table

in the window, Qwilleran said, "We talked about this earlier, but may I ask again your impression of how the residents of Hibbard House reacted to Alden's presence and Violet's rather sudden marriage?"

"Well . . . as I said, to tell the truth, Qwill, things had been changing in recent weeks — one of the reasons I decided to leave. There had been a wonderful family feeling before. Violet was such a gracious hostess. But after Alden arrived she let him take over selecting the menus and the evening's entertainment. Alden took charge of the wine cellar and assumed full responsibility of Tasso, the watchdog. I know he's very fond of dogs, but the rest of us enjoyed walking Tasso in our turn. . . . So the marriage wasn't a complete shock, just a disappointment. The girls thought Judd Amhurst would have been more suitable. . . . I still don't know if I should be telling you all this —"

"Have no qualms, Connie. I ask simply because I care about the gallant old house I'm assigned to document." Qwilleran said, "As you know, I'm doing the text for a book on the Hibbard House. Can you think of any anecdotes that might be included?"

"Not offhand, but I'll think about it."

"Has Alden Wade made any difference to the lifestyle?"

"Well . . . he plays the piano, and we've had a few Sunday-night songfests that were fun. He can cook, and he taught our housekeeper how to make duck à l'orange. And I hear they've had some all-night card games in the men's quarters. . . . If I think of more, I'll let you know."

Early in the evening, Qwilleran had a phone call from Hixie Rice, promotion director for the *Something*. The quality of the transmission indicated she was using her cell phone on the shoulder of a busy highway.

"Qwill, are you going to be there for a few minutes? I've been asked to deliver a small package to you."

"Who asked? Do you know the person? Does it look suspicious?"

"You indefatigable joker!" she said with a delighted laugh. "The copyboy asked me to deliver a tape recording. He says you're in a hurry to get it."

"Come along. Can you stay for a drink?"

"Not this time, thanks. I'm having dinner with . . . a rather attractive business contact."

"I'm sure!"

Within minutes she parked at the curb, leaving the motor running, and ran up the walk with hair flying, full skirt swirling. Hixie was always in a state of contagious excitement.

She handed over the tape and dashed back to her car, stopping only to call out, "Sesquicentennial committee meets at the hotel Friday evening. You're welcome to attend."

Then she was gone, leaving Kenneth's tape and a whiff of expensive perfume. Pickax had been scheduled to celebrate its sesquicentennial this summer, until it was discovered that someone (possibly Hixie) had miscalculated the dates. It was just as well, Qwilleran thought. A new bookstore and Dundee — plus a sesquicentennial — would have been too much for a city the size of Pickax.

He went immediately to the tape player and heard a raspy voice tell the following tale:

My name is Helen Wentley. I heard this awful tale many times when I was growing up. My ancestors came here from Finland to work in the mines. My grandmother was housekeeper for the Hibbards, and she told how they were snowbound for three weeks in that big

house on the hill. There were no telephones then, for them to call for help
— and no snowplows, that's for sure.

Where shall I begin? It was called the
worst snowstorm in the history of
Moose County. It was about a hundred
years ago.

When it struck, everyone huddled
around the many fireplaces and told
stories. But it kept on snowing — and
snowing. The big house got colder and
colder. They had to conserve firewood.
So Mr. Hibbard decided they should all
live in the library, easiest room to heat.
That meant four Hibbards and
Grandma, the handyman, and a house-
maid.

Grandma had to figure out how to
cook in the fireplace. She said they had
a lot of soup and oatmeal. The hired
man kept bringing in firewood, but the
woodpile was running low, and they
ended up — before the storm was over
— chopping up furniture and even
burning books!

They brought pillows and blankets
into the library and slept on the floor.
In daytime they wore hats and coats
and leggings. Mr. Hibbard read aloud.
Mrs. Hibbard got everyone singing

songs and playing guessing games.

After a while food was running low. There were laying hens and a milk cow in the barn, and there was a lot of canned fruit in the cellar. It got harder and harder to dig through the drifting snow. And everyone was getting sick from eating so much fruit and oatmeal — if you know what I mean.

So Mr. Hibbard decided they should butcher the cow and chickens for food. They had no feed and would only freeze to death. That's what happened to the horses. They froze to death.

When somebody suggested bringing the horses into the parlor, they all laughed themselves silly. Grandma said they were beginning to crack up.

That's when the handyman decided to tramp into town on homemade snowshoes — in search of help. It was seven miles, and it was still snowing. He was never heard from again, but his body was found during the spring thaw.

And still it snowed — and snowed. Even Mr. Hibbard was discouraged. Grandma said, "I think we should pray." He was not a religious person, but they all prayed.

And then a miracle happened, according to Grandma. A small church in Kennebeck sent out search parties to rescue folks in out-of-the-way cabins and farmhouses, and a sudden inspiration directed them to the big house on the hill.

Qwilleran was impressed. He went to the phone to call the young man but decided to wait until after the dinner hour. Kenneth would be potlucking with his peers at the Winston Park apartments. Peggy had said it was one of the things they did twice a week.

So it was nine o'clock before Qwilleran phoned. To his surprise the operator said, "This number is no longer in service."

On the other hand, it was not surprising. Kenneth had probably moved in with another tenant to share expenses. Which one, and why, was a question not worth considering.

Still, Qwilleran felt a tremor on his upper lip, and he pounded his moustache with his fist.

Then he shouted, "Read!" and Koko came running. He bounded to a bookshelf without stopping to make a decision and knocked down George Ade's *Fables in Slang*.

When Qwilleran phoned Polly at eleven o'clock, his first words were "What do you know about George Ade?"

"American humorist," she said. "Turn of the last century."

"Once a librarian, always a librarian," he said.

TWENTY-TWO

 On Wednesday morning Qwilleran fed the cats and recited a few lines of Rudyard Kipling as their thought for the day. He himself had a bowl of cereal with a sliced banana, followed by the obligatory cup of coffee.

Thus fortified, he called the city room at the paper and asked to speak to Whiskers.

"He doesn't work here anymore," said the deskman.

"Since when?" was the shocked response.

"Since yesterday."

"What happened?"

"I don't know. Talk to the boss."

Qwilleran sat down with a second cup of coffee and reflected: Was he fired? Did he quit? In either case, what was the reason? Was he in trouble? Had he blurted out too many secrets and suspicions while under the influence of Squunk water and a sympathetic listener?

Qwilleran phoned the managing editor.

"Junior! What happened to Whiskers?"

"He quit to go back to school."

"So suddenly?"

"Well, you know . . . these young kids don't know which way is up."

"Did he leave a forwarding address? I owe him for some legwork he did."

"No address. He'll probably send you a bill. How about running copy for us until we can hire a replacement?"

"You couldn't afford me."

Hanging up abruptly, Qwilleran next called Peggy at the Winston Park apartments. "This is Qwill. What happened to your neighbor with the whiskers?"

"I don't know. I had a dinner date with — guess who! — Wetherby Goode! We went to — guess where! — the Palomino Paddock! And when I got home, there was a note from Kenneth asking me to turn in his rental car and collect what you owe him for his research assignment. Does that make sense?"

"I understand that, but what I don't understand is why. Did he leave an address?"

"Nothing! I thought you and Ken had a good working arrangement."

"We did, and he did good work. So his defection comes as a surprise. Let me know what expenses need to be covered.

How did you like the Palomino Paddock?"

"Super! Wetherby said it was informal, and I expected some kind of hayseed operation, but it was quite classy in spite of all the horsy atmosphere."

Qwilleran had met Judd Amhurst briefly at Hibbard House one evening, and they had exchanged the fraternal handshake of Squunkers. A growing number of thirsty citizens of Moose County were adopting the local mineral water as their drink of choice.

Now Connie suggested Judd as the best source of contemporary trivia about the Big House on the Hill.

So Qwilleran phoned and invited him to the Village for an afternoon of memories about Hibbard House. As Qwilleran recalled, he was a retired engineer, distinguished by a crop of snow-white hair. It was not as full and rampant as that of Thornton Haggis, but it had the same kind of attraction for Koko and Yum Yum.

They met him in the foyer of Unit Four, with tails waving.

Judd asked, "Are these the two characters who write the 'Qwill Pen' column?"

"The secret is out! I hope it won't go any

further. Have you visited Indian Village before?"

"I've attended a couple of meetings of the bird club, and once I gave a talk on the birds of the Hibbard estate. It took a lot of research, but I enjoyed it."

Qwilleran said, "It sounds like data that could be used in the book. Do you have your notes?"

"Better yet, the bird club taped my remarks, and a transcription should be available."

They sat in the two lounge sofas, facing each other across the opulent pile rug.

"It's even shaggier than Alden's," Judd said. "His sitting room is quite modern."

Then he explained that the four male residents had quarters in a stone guest house down the hill from the main building.

"Cyrus, the first Hibbard, was in the sawyer business and was infatuated with wood — which is all very well, but his descendants have lived in fear of fire ever after."

Qwilleran said, "I'd like to tape this."

The following account was recorded:

Violet's grandfather, Geoffrey, was educated at schools in New England and abroad and was a highly social creature. He would invite his whole fraternity up in the summer, a few at a time. They would arrive by train, which had replaced the stagecoach. They would spend a couple of weeks, housed in a guest house of quarry stone that Geoffrey built down the hill on the edge of a picturesque pond. It was a common frog pond, and the bullfrogs kept the guests awake with their amorous croaking. He had given the elegant guest house a snooty French name, but waggish guests changed it to the Froggery, and frog legs à la Provençal were frequently on the menu.

Dinners were black-tie every night, Violet said, with music by a string trio, footmen to serve, and a butler to pour.

But the twentieth century was making life more casual, and her father, Jesmore, was more interested in literature than entertaining, so the Froggery was boarded up. It came to life only when Violet inherited — with a new name. Alden called it the Old Rock Pile.

The facilities are fantastic. Each of our suites has a sitting room lavishly furnished, and a whirlpool bath. Evenings in the main house are made very special by Violet's hospitality. . . . That's the story!

Qwilleran turned off the tape recorder and asked, "Are you a duck hunter like the others?"

"No. I'm a bookworm. What attracted me to the residence was the extensive library. Violet gave a lot of books to ESP, but there are hundreds remaining — not current bestsellers but famous oldies, like *Portrait of a Lady* and *Mill on the Floss*.

"What I like about Alden is that he can discuss books. I've never known anyone else who shared my particular interest. Otherwise, we watch sports on TV and play cards."

Qwilleran inquired politely if Alden's marriage had put a crimp in Ping-Pong tournaments, card games, and so on.

"No," he said. "She's quite a bit older, you know, and not in the best of health, they say, so she retires early and Alden can stay up playing Ping-Pong or pinochle.

"And speaking of ESP, as we were, I was a Saturday regular at Edd Smith's shop. I spent a lot of time on his ladder and bought a lot of sardines for Winston. Your speech at the lit club brought it all back."

The two men gazed into space for a few moments until Qwilleran asked, "How did the residents at Hibbard House react to Violet's sudden marriage?"

"We all said the right things, but no one said what he was really thinking. Alden's a good guy — talented and all that — but he comes on a little strong. . . . I'm talking more than I should. Don't quote me."

"Have no fear. This is merely local color . . . for my ears only! What I need now is the kind of folklore that's soaked up in the woodwork of old buildings, myths and mysteries."

"I'll scout around. Violet's father left a diary —"

"Perfect!"

"I'll ask her if I can see it . . . and even if she says I can't, I know where it is."

He stood up to leave, and the Siamese — who had been listening to his every word for reasons of their own — stepped aside to let him pass.

"Nice cats!" he said.

"They're on their best behavior. You should be here when a big storm is coming and they go bananas!"

"Do you let them out?"

"Never!"

"That's good," Judd said. "There are

coyotes in the woods this year."

Late in the afternoon, Qwilleran felt thumping vibrations coming through the wall to the north. The Siamese felt it, too, and stared at the wall. He knew what they did not know — Wetherby was rehearsing a piano number to play just before his six-o'clock weather forecast.

When the thumping stopped, Qwilleran phoned his neighbor. "Joe, do you require a booster shot before tonight's program?"

"I'll hop over there!"

"Bring your saltshaker and feather."

Koko and Yum Yum met him at the door. They knew he lived with Jet Stream. Drinks were served, and the two men sat in facing sofas, while the cats took up positions on the pile rug.

The host began. "It has been reported that you were seen at the Palomino Paddock, disporting with an unidentified female. What do you have to say for yourself?"

"What are you? A policeman? I never disport! I don't even know what it means. Your operatives have me confused with someone else. Actually, I was there with the girl you introduced me to and we had an agreeable time, except that she comes on heavy with computer-fab. She wanted

255

me to buy one. I told her I prefer the piano."

"What's your theme song for tonight? Since they soundproofed the walls, I have to wait for the program."

Wetherby burst into song: "There's no sun up in the sky! Stormy weather!"

Hearing the booming voice, both cats levitated and shot from the room.

"Thanks a lot!" he shouted after them. "Seriously, Qwill, we're in for a rough time. Stock up on firewood, flashlight batteries, bottled water, and canned soup."

At eleven o'clock Qwilleran and Polly enjoyed their traditional telephone nightcap.

She had found a recipe for mulligatawny. He was reading Mencken. She was thinking of buying a new winter coat. He had kidded Joe about "disporting" with an unidentified female. They both said a lingering "*à bientôt.*"

After that Qwilleran fell asleep promptly and slept soundly until almost one a.m. when his bedside telephone rang loudly and urgently, or so it seemed to a sleep-befuddled mind. He growled something incoherent into the mouthpiece.

A woman's voice sobbed, "Forgive me,

Qwill, for calling so late. This is Maggie. I have sad news. I had to tell someone."

"That's all right, Maggie. What has happened?"

"We've lost our dear Violet!" There was a torrent of sobbing.

This was the phone call he expected to receive eventually, but not so soon. "Sad news indeed," he murmured.

"They called me a half hour ago. It was inevitable. But now that it's happened, I'm in shock! I don't know how to deal with it. We were like sisters."

"Just cry, Maggie. Tears are a great healer, so don't be afraid to cry your eyes out. When you can cry no more, you'll feel a great calm, and then you'll think of a way to honor Violet's memory."

"You're right, Qwill. That's exactly what Jeremy would have said." Her voice trailed off, and he thought he heard a heart-rending wail before she hung up.

His advice was based on experience, and he knew it would work. He imagined her five "ladies" gathering around to comfort her, as all cats know how to do. The Siamese sensed something was amiss, and they were whimpering outside his door. He opened it and let them in.

TWENTY-THREE

 Qwilleran thought about Violet on Thursday morning as he fed the cats and himself (in that order). He thought about her ingratiating personality and intelligence and love of poetry and drama. He thought about her shattered romance in early years and her strange marriage in later life. He hesitated to call it a romance. Yet who could tell? And what would happen now? Whatever . . . he felt driven to complete the book. He could imagine the pleasure it would have given her; the photographs of cozy corners, family treasures, and architectural wonders. The text, he was sure, would have delighted her. That was what he had to concentrate on now, relating historic incidents with affection and humor rather than journalistic objectivity. In other words, he planned to write what she would have liked to read. He would dedicate the book simply "To Violet." And there would be a handsome photograph of her, selected from the Hibbard archives with the aid of Maggie.

But first he had things to do. High on the list was Polly's grocery shopping. He had a key to her condo, enabling him to refrigerate perishables. And he had a standing invitation to a pickup dinner of leftovers as a reward for his kindness. There were always errands for him to do at the bank, post office, and drugstore as well as at Toodle's Market. And on this occasion he had an urge to visit Andy Brodie.

The police department was in the rear of the City Hall building, up one flight.

The sergeant on the desk waved Qwilleran through the gate and toward the glass-enclosed office where the chief could be seen growling at the computer.

"Come in, laddie! Rest your bones!" the chief barked in a Scots accent. "How's the rugged life in the wilderness?"

"I miss our spur-of-the-moment nightcaps, Andy. The cats miss you, too. Koko wants me to ask you if the Lockmaster sniping case was ever closed."

"Nope."

"There was something about a member of the family being involved — on the grapevine, that is. Was that ever under investigation?"

"Yep. It was dropped for lack of evidence. They had to go easy because he was a prominent citizen."

"Apparently the situation in Lockmaster became too unfriendly; the prominent citizen moved to Moose County. Did you know that?"

"Yep."

"He's made a big hit here. In fact, he married the older woman who's the sole heir to the four-generation Hibbard fortune. I'm sure you know that. It was in the paper last Friday."

"Yep."

"The bride died early this morning," Qwilleran said. "There'll be a bulletin on the front page today. Cause of death: brain aneurysm."

"*Och, mon!* What does your smart cat think about this hanky-panky?"

"Well, the man has been to the barn twice, and both times Koko was conspicuous by his absence. The second time Koko arranged for him to slip on a banana peel. You figure it out!"

Arriving home at the Willows, Qwilleran realized that the condo offered Koko a greater showcase for his talents than the barn had ever done. Instead of a single kitchen window in which to prance, he had three. There was a tall narrow sidelight alongside the front door. The dining ell, which served as writing studio as well, had a horizontal window with a wide ledge. The kitchen had another horizontal window above the sink counter.

When Qwilleran drove up, Koko was performing in all three windows — not easy to do, but he was a fast operator. His agitation indicated messages on the answering machine, which turned out to be from Lisa Compton, Burgess Campbell, the Lanspeaks, and others — friends wanting to talk to friends in a moment of mourning.

Qwilleran first returned the call from Maggie.

"Oh, Qwill! Thank you so much for what you said last night. Today I feel a blessed calm and a resolve to do something constructive."

"Good! Is there anything I can do to help?"

"Your help with a memorial service would be much appreciated. I'm Violet's executor, and I want to plan a tribute she would approve of. I wondered if you would deliver the eulogy. You have such a wonderful voice and such a compelling presence."

"Don't get carried away, Maggie. I think

someone like Burgess Campbell would be more suitable. His family has known her family for generations, and he and she worked together on the board of ESP. His lectures at the college are outstanding for content and style, not to mention that chesty Scottish voice. And with Alexander by his side, it would make a moving farewell to a dear friend. Violet liked dogs, you know."

"Perfect! Perfect! I'm so glad I talked with you, Qwill."

"One more thought, Maggie. Poetry and drama were Violet's great loves. Readings from great writers would be highly appropriate. Polly could read one or two of Byron's shorter works, and I'd consider it a privilege to deliver a passage from Shakespeare."

Later that afternoon a phone call came from Alden Wade. Qwilleran offered the bereaved husband condolences with a promise to pursue the book project with renewed dedication — as a tribute to a wonderful woman.

"It's a genuine expression of my feelings. Is there anything I can do?" Qwilleran asked.

"I'd like to tell you about a conversation

Violet and I had during our last afternoon together. Would you have a few minutes?"

"By all means. We're living at Indian Village now."

He gave Alden instructions for reaching the Willows and gave Koko instructions in how to behave.

"The poor guy has just lost his wife, Koko! Try to show some warmth, some understanding."

Koko crept away with head and tail lowered and was not seen for the next few hours.

When Alden arrived, Qwilleran gripped his hand with feeling and ushered him to one of the loungy sofas.

The guest declined refreshments and launched into his report: "You probably know that Violet's grandfather liked to entertain. He's the one who built the lavish guest house down the hill in the rear. It's now referred to as the Old Rock Pile — affectionately, not disrespectfully. His guests would stay two weeks or more, enjoying the outdoors during the day, then dressing up and reporting to the main house for a formal dinner and an evening of table games. Are you a card player, Qwill?"

"I'm afraid not. As a kid I played a yelling, screaming, table-thumping card game called Pit, but that's all."

"Well, Geoffrey offered his guests a Games Gallery with a choice of a hundred table games — everything from chess to mah-jongg. The young people had a choice of Old Maid, Flinch, Chinese checkers, and the like. Old-timers could play dominoes or whist. There was backgammon, Parcheesi, Monopoly — everything. This was between 1900 and 1950, you know."

"It sounds as if you have a museum there, Alden."

"That's what Violet said. Even the regular playing cards are in beautiful boxes: carved, hand-painted, or inlaid with mother-of-pearl. She thought a description of the gallery could be included in the text, but you'd have to see it."

"Gladly! How about tomorrow?"

Arrangements were made. Alden went on his way. And Koko came sneaking out from underneath the sofa.

"What's wrong with you?" Qwilleran demanded.

Arriving at Polly's for dinner that evening, Qwilleran was met by Brutus, the security guard, and Catta, who had the manner of a shy hoyden.

They supervised while he set up the butterfly table along the window wall, laid it with two place settings, selected the dinner music, and fixed the cat food. Then Polly served a casserole of mixed leftovers (his not to question what) enhanced by a sprinkling of parsley and toasted almonds.

While the music system played Chopin nocturnes, they discussed the approaching weather (stormy) and the newly questioned status of Dundee.

"You see," Polly said, "people come in to see him and they end up buying a book. The Green Smocks swear that Dundee's professional charm accounts for fifty percent of purchases. Tax-wise, that means we can take his food, litter, valet services, and vet fees as business expenses. Or we can make him a salaried employee and let him pay for his own upkeep and health insurance. In that case, should he have his own Social Security number and file a tax return?"

She seemed quite serious about it, so he replied seriously, "I'd hate to see the bookstore or Dundee get into trouble. Ask your accountant to take it up with the Internal Revenue Service."

After dinner they turned off the music and discussed readings for Violet's memorial service.

Polly said she might read Byron's short poem "She Walks in Beauty, Like the Night."

Qwilleran said Violet reminded him of Portia in *The Merchant of Venice*. He could read her famous oration: *The quality of mercy is not strain'd.*

It was the kind of bookish evening they both enjoyed — the kind that had been missing from their lives during Polly's indoctrination in the book business.

All at once there was a flash of electric blue that lighted the night sky surrounding the Willows. It illuminated the interior for half a second through the window wall.

"Sheet lightning," Qwilleran said. "Joe has been predicting violent weather for the last couple of days. I'd better walk home before we get a drenching downpour."

As he walked toward Unit Four, a van pulled up alongside the curb, and Wetherby Goode called out, "Want a lift?" He was on his way home from his eleven-o'clock stint at WPKX.

"Want a nightcap? After your hard work on the airwaves," Qwilleran retorted.

"Thanks. I'll stable my horse and bounce right over there." The sky flashed electric blue again. "Sheet lightning," he said.

In a few minutes he reported to Unit Four. "Where are the cats?"

"Koko's upstairs predicting the weather. He plans to apply for your job. Yum Yum's under the sofa. She doesn't care for lightning."

"Who does? I gave a talk on lightning at the clubhouse last year and asked how many people enjoy electrical storms. Not one hand went up. A few said they found thunderstorms exciting, provided it wasn't too loud and one had something to drink!"

"Is it true that you shouldn't stand under a tree during an electrical storm?"

"Absolutely! Lightning goes for tall targets. Trees are tall. The intense heat boils the sap and explodes the tree."

"One more question, Joe. What exactly is sheet lightning?"

"Sometimes the lightning flash is obscured by clouds, which are then brightly illuminated. During sheet lightning, the flash seems to come from everywhere, lighting up the whole sky. That's what we've been getting for the last hour. . . . But enough of that. I learned something electrifying in Horseradish this week. I raced over there for a birthday party following my forecast, and I met the girl who was going to marry Ronnie Dickson this fall. You remember his fatal accident, Qwill?"

"I remember. The official report blamed the use of drugs plus alcohol."

"Well, according to this girl, Alden Wade was the one who suggested uppers to Ronnie, saying they were in common use for stage fright. She and her friends think Alden wanted to get rid of Ronnie. There was a whispering campaign in Horseradish about the sniping of Mrs. Wade. Alden's stepson and Ronnie were the instigators. No one knows what happened to the stepson, but Ronnie sure is out of the picture."

"Interesting," Qwilleran said. "Do you buy that story, Joe?"

"Well . . . she's an intelligent girl — very serious, very sincere. Thanks for the drink, Qwill." He jumped up. "Gotta get home and talk to Jetboy. He's a big, strong tomcat, but when there's an electrical storm, I have to sit and hold his paw."

"Does you credit, Joe," Qwilleran said as he accompanied his neighbor to the front door.

When he returned, Koko and Yum Yum were sitting in the middle of the floor, regarding him intently. Their bedtime snack was past due.

TWENTY-FOUR

Qwilleran marched the Siamese up to their sleeping room on the balcony, said goodnight, and closed the door. The latter was merely an end-of-the-day gesture; Koko could open the door whenever he felt like going downstairs to watch the nightlife on the riverbank.

In the adjoining quarters, Qwilleran completed his bedtime ablutions and was settling down for a few pages of the *Wilson Quarterly* before lights-out, when he heard a crash downstairs and the sounds of a minor riot! He rushed up to the balcony railing and heard snarling and growling.

Qwilleran's first thought was that Koko had teased a coyote into crashing through the window wall and creating panic . . . but no! It was only Koko having a cat fit, as he always did before a major storm. He swooped around and around, knocking down lamps, decorative objects, side chairs, kitchen utensils, and everything on Qwilleran's writing table.

"Koko! No!" he thundered in a voice intended to slow the cat down. Koko went on looking for havoc to create.

"Treat!" came the magic word. Koko went on rolling in the lush pile of the shag rug that was now littered with salted almonds from the nut bowl.

There were distant rolls of thunder and one loud roar ending in a frightening *crack!* like a battery of rifle shots.

Koko calmly stood up, using a luxurious shudder to divest his fur of salt. Then he walked calmly upstairs, leaving Qwilleran to clean up the mess.

The man was in no mood to tidy the place thoroughly at that hour. He straightened furniture and a few kitchen utensils and shook his head over the rugful of salted nuts. But it was late. He was tired. The Siamese were both in their room, and he retired to his own room.

Claps of thunder were punctuating the growing rumble and roar in the western sky. Bolts of lightning forked down from the clouds. Through his upstairs window there was a panorama of electrical turbulence such as Qwilleran had never seen. Once, a huge ball of fire seemed to bounce across the distant treetops as if looking for a lofty target. Awed by the scene, he hardly heard the police sirens. But he saw a sudden burst of light in the midnight sky, and he heard the honk-honk of fire trucks approaching from two, then three directions! His blood chilled. Lightning sought the highest target! Out there to the northwest was the Big House on the Hill!

He turned on his shortwave radio and heard a squeaking voice ". . . fire at the Hibbard estate on West Kennebeck Road. Firefighters from four communities responding . . ."

Qwilleran's sole reaction was: Thank God Violet didn't live to see this happen!

He slept hardly at all that night. The Siamese stole quietly into his room to give the solace they seemed to know was needed.

The glow in the sky continued after the thunder and lightning faded away. There was no one he could call in the middle of the night, and no one called him until six-thirty a.m.

An urgent voice said, "Qwill, this is Junior. Did you hear —"

"Yes, I heard."

"We're getting out an Extra. Early deadline. Could you come downtown to help?"

Qwilleran dressed in a hurry, skipped his

coffee, threw some dry food in the cats' plates, and drove to the news office. Whatever they wanted him to do would help staunch the emotions that flooded his mind.

He wrote a description of the house, wrote cutlines for Bushland's photos, and suggested someone who might supply information.

When the edition hit the street, the news covered the front page and the picture page. The banner headline was . . .

HISTORIC MANSION BURNS TO GROUND

And a sidebar was headed:

HERO KILLED TRYING TO RESCUE DOG

As soon as the newspaper was put to bed, Qwilleran went directly home, avoiding the town gossips — whose information had come from WPKX or the grapevine.

At home he erased all messages on his answering machine, except one. The others, he decided, could call again or buy a newspaper. The only person he wanted to talk with was Judd Amhurst. He had recommended Judd to the editor as the best source of personal information. Now he phoned his private number at the Old Rock Pile. When old Geoffrey Hibbard built it a century before, down the hill from the main house, little did he know that it would be the only remaining structure when all else had burned.

Judd arrived at the Willows looking ten years older than he did before the fire. Qwilleran himself felt ten years older.

They shook hands solemnly, forgetting to use the fraternal handshake, and the guest chose coffee instead of Squunk water.

Qwilleran waved him toward one of the sofas. "Make yourself comfortable."

Judd was carrying a briefcase, which he placed on the coffee table. He said, "It's good to get away for an hour or so. The sight of that mountain of ashes makes me ill. It's depressing to be a witness to the end of something.

"In the Old Rock Pile last night, we'd been playing cards and were ready to call it a day when there was a deafening thunderclap and a blinding flash of lightning. It sounded too close! We jumped up from the table and ran outside. Then it sounded like an explosion! Alden called nine-one-one. We could see flames. We ran up the hill. All kinds of sirens were screaming! Suddenly Alden yelled, 'The dog! The dog! The dog!' Tasso was shut up in a room next to the kitchen. We tried to stop Alden but he sprinted for the burning house, shouting the dog's name! The firefighters yelled at him, but he kept on going. . . . That was the last we saw of him. The paper said both Alden and the dog probably died of smoke inhalation, but the two of them burned along with that old, wooden relic."

Qwilleran said, "You must have been absolutely stunned!"

Judd nodded. "We couldn't think. We couldn't talk with any sense. We certainly couldn't sleep, but we were penned up in the Old Rock Pile because the air was filled with smoke. The Wix boys found a bottle in Alden's room and proceeded to knock themselves out. I looked at his bookcase for something that might take my mind off the disaster. And that's when I saw a title that jolted me back to my senses."

Judd reached for the briefcase and unclasped it.

"There was a copy of Hemingway's *Death in the Afternoon*! That is the rare book that was stolen from the ESP!"

"But thousands have been printed over

the years," Qwilleran reminded him.

"Yes, but this copy was autographed and a first edition . . . and inside the back cover was the ESP sticker with catalogue number!" He drew it from the briefcase and handed it over.

Qwilleran looked at the sticker and murmured, "What can I say? It's hard to believe that Alden would steal it and then report it stolen!"

"The question is — what do I do with it? I was brought up to believe that you never speak ill of the dead. I can't return it to the ESP without telling where I found it."

"Mail it back anonymously, Judd, preferably from a Lockmaster or Bixby post office. I have a book mailer you can use."

"Thanks, Qwill. I knew you'd have a solution."

"Meanwhile, where are the three of you staying?"

"The Wix boys are going back with their parents. I'm going to check into the motel in Kennebeck. Violet's attorney is sending someone to pick up our keys and take responsibility for the Old Rock Pile and its contents. I never want to see it again!"

 During their nightly phone chat, Qwilleran and Polly grieved over the

Hibbard House tragedy and expressed shock over the Alden Wade sacrifice.

Polly said, "I knew he was a dog fancier. He ignored Dundee, and he often mentioned Violet's hound, an Italian breed I've never heard of."

"I can understand his desperation to save Tasso," Qwilleran said. "I believe I'd do the same if Koko and Yum Yum were penned inside a burning building."

"I don't know how we'll replace Alden. He did a good job of managing special events, except for the proposed story hour for children. He didn't feel comfortable with youngsters."

"And I doubt whether they'd be comfortable with him, Polly. I could suggest a successor. He's retired, an avid reader, a member of the lit club, a longtime customer of Edd Smith, and a grandfather with white hair. Kids would warm up to him. His name is Judd Amhurst. You can reach him at the Kennebeck Motel."

"*À bientôt,* dear, and thank you."

"*À bientôt.*"

Qwilleran repaired to his office in the dining ell to work on his personal journal. He wrote with an old gold fountain pen for sentimental reasons and because it flowed well, although it had to be kept under wraps when Yum Yum was around. She and Koko were behind closed doors on the balcony, enjoying their beauty sleep.

Friday, October 10 — A day that will live in memory and a mystery that will never be solved publicly. Who stole the rare book from ESP and returned it anonymously? And who was the sniper who killed Alden's first wife? There will be guesses and gossip ad infinitum.

Malicious talk always circulates around people who are too successful, too proper, too talented, too well spoken, too well dressed, and too-too-much.

A.W. was all of these. Questions will buzz around like flies, and answers will be given with lifted eyebrows and wise smirks. What was behind the brief marriage of Violet and A.W.? Why did his first wife marry him so soon after her husband's suicide? Was it really suicide? Did Ronnie Dickson take uppers of his own accord, or did A.W. suggest them? And why . . . ?

What would Polly say if she knew about Alden and the stolen book? She would probably quote her father:

There's a little good in the worst of us, and a little bad in the best of us.

Makes one wonder if he's guilty of the other crimes pinned on him by the gossips. Makes one wonder if Koko sensed something wrong about the guy.

How about Koko's sudden interest in certain Shakespeare plays: Hamlet's mother married too soon after her husband's death; Othello killed his wife.

And how about Koko's interest in *Fables in Slang* by George Ade? Alden's real name was George Wade! That would be an amusing coincidence if you took it seriously. I know Koko's track record, and, frankly, all of this makes my hair stand on end.

Enough of this! I'm getting punchy!

"Yow!" came a howl too close to Qwilleran's ear for comfort. Koko had opened his bedroom door, crept stealthily downstairs, and leapt noiselessly to the back of Qwilleran's chair, where he was now teetering.

"What are you doing down here?" Qwilleran demanded.

Koko sprang to the table and sat on a stack of papers in a ready-for-business pose.

His presence brought back many a recollection. Koko had shown a pointed dislike of Alden by avoiding him. And he had gone one slippery step further — one slippery step, on a banana peel!

Qwilleran closed his journal.

"Okay," he said to Koko. "Let's see what we can find in the kitchen."

He poured some Kabbibbles into the cats' plates and had a large dish of ice cream for himself.

About the Author

Lilian Jackson Braun is the author of twenty-seven *Cat Who* novels and three short story collections.